The Virtu...
Series/Book Three

Backfire

A Novel

William Kritlow

Publishers Since 1798

THOMAS NELSON PUBLISHERS
Nashville • Atlanta • London • Vancouver

Published in Nashville, Tennessee, by Thomas Nelson, Inc., Publishers,
and distributed in Canada by Word Communications, Ltd., Richmond,
British Columbia, and in the United Kingdom by Word (UK), Ltd., Milton
Keynes, England.

Scripture quotations are from the NEW KING JAMES VERSION of the
Bible. Copyright © 1979, 1980, 1982, Thomas Nelson, Inc., Publishers.

Library of Congress-in-Publication Data

Kritlow, William
    Backfire : a novel / William Kritlow.
        p. cm. — (The virtual reality series ; bk. 3)
    Summary: Like Satan's attempts to lure away God's children, a twisted
plot in virtual reality threatens Tim when he is caught in his own
computer program.
    ISBN 0-7852-7925-3
    [1. Virtual reality—Fiction. 2. Christian life Fiction. 3. Comput-
ers—Fiction. 4. Brothers and sisters—Fiction. 5. Science fiction.] I.
Title. II. Series: Kritlow, William. Virtual reality series ; bk. 3.
PZ7.K914Bah   1995
[Fic]—dc20   95-7883
                                                                        CIP
                                                                         AC

Printed in the United States of America
1 2 3 4 5 6 7 - 01 00 99 98 97 96 95

C H A P T E R 1

Do you think it'll work?" Kelly asked Tim as they both climbed into their Virtual Reality suits. The VR suits were made of a black material made bulky by a thick mesh of wires, sensors, sensation producers, and other gadgets.

"It'll work—" Tim said. "I think."

Ready to zip up the suit and bring the visor down, Kelly grinned. "This will be good."

"Better than good," Tim said, excitement charging his voice. "Wait till you see what's waiting for us."

"So this is where you disappeared to yesterday."

"I like to program more than you do."

"You're just faster. I think about what I'm doing more carefully."

"Yeah, right."

Tim and Kelly had been programming Matthew Helbert's Virtual Reality machine for the past few weeks. They had succeeded in creating several virtual places and some small adventures, but nothing as complicated as what they were about to enter. They wanted these programs to work more than ever. What they had created this time was special—they had programmed their living dreams.

As the helmet visors came down and their VR suit zippers locked in place, an anxious excitement surged through them both.

They were not disappointed.

The inside of their visors came alive. The computer painted the world they saw in brilliant colors thirty times a second—so fast and with such perfect definition that what was being painted before their eyes became all the reality they knew.

"Great!" Tim exclaimed. "Just what I programmed." A cool spring morning arose around them; birds chirped, and there was a steady rustle of leaves.

"With hot summer outside," Kelly said, remembering the hay she had just finished stacking in the hot barn, "this is a real relief." But the weather was secondary to what glistened before them—two sleek, black Harley-Davidson motorcycles!

"You're kidding!" she exclaimed. "We're going to ride these?"

"Come on. It'll be cool."

Kelly walked cautiously up to one bike and ran her hand over the seat, then over the gas tank.

"I digitized it from a brochure I got in town," Tim explained as he, too, placed appreciative hands on the gas tank and ran them along the seat. He caressed the chrome light and ran a loving hand along the handlebars. It didn't matter that it wasn't real; it looked real and felt real.

"It really feels like a Harley," Kelly said, still apprehensive.

"Ready?" Tim climbed aboard, kicked up the stand, and then pushed the starter. Now it sounded real. The engine roared to life—musical thunder. Tim cranked the throttle. The bike roared, power crying up from the engine.

Kelly eyed her brother hesitantly. It wasn't as bad as flying, but motorcycles were still dangerous. *But this isn't real, right? This is like in the arcades,* she reminded herself. Overcoming her reluctance, she swung her leg over, settled into the large, comfortable leather seat, and pushed the starter. The growl shuddered through her.

Knowing he was leading the way, Tim eased forward, slowly at first, getting used to the feel. He circled Kelly as she throttled the engine, kicked the kickstand up, and also eased forward. Both had ridden bicycles and horses, but this was far different. It took a moment to get used to it. But only a moment.

The instant a sense of confidence took hold, Kelly punched the throttle. The engine whined and leaped forward, and moments later she had caught up to Tim. Together they roared down the road.

"What do you think?" Tim called to her over the insistent growl.

"Wow!" she cried back. The motorcycle might be virtual, but the thrill was real. "But what if we fall?"

"We can't. I've programmed it that way. We're invincible. That's why no helmets."

The countryside flew past them in a blur. They leaned forward, their eyes riveted to the road ahead, the sensation just as they had imagined it would be. There was only one difference. If they had really been riding Harleys, the wind would be pressing their faces, bruising their eyes. But the visor kept the suit from simulating all that. It actually made driving at high speed more fun.

Tim cranked it up and pulled ahead. Kelly did the same and pulled alongside him.

"I feel so free," Tim cried.

"It's because cows can't go this fast," Kelly joked.

Tim laughed, but he actually was beginning to feel invincible—powerful. He could go as fast as he wanted and never be hurt. And the Virtual Reality machine simulated the experience wonderfully. He *was* invincible. He couldn't fall—he'd programmed it that way. He couldn't run into anything—he'd programmed it *that* way. He could only surge forward, covering more and more ground, and as he did his power grew and, with it, his freedom.

With the increased speed, Kelly needed her full concentration to keep the motorcycle on the road. While she hunched forward, afraid to blink, Tim glanced casually from side to side. They were passing a lake on his right, a long glistening patch of blue surrounded by budding oak and maple trees, sweet with early spring. Tim loved it. He had only told the computer that the time was spring, and the computer had done the rest. What else awaited them up ahead?

This was awesome! He was leaving the hard work of the farm behind and going anywhere he wanted—if a place wasn't in VR now, he could program it and put it there. The possibilities were endless.

They slowed, swerved around a curve, leaning into it and accelerating—the trees became a blur of green again.

"When do we get to where we're going?" Kelly called to him.

"I thought you'd want a long ride first."

"I've got something special waiting for me in my own program."

"How about a race?"

Before she could say no an alarm went off—two words flashing at the lower right corner of both visors: "Get me—get me."

The "me" referred to Uncle Morty.

The last time Uncle Morty had gone into Chippewa Falls, the nearest town to his Wisconsin farm, he had seen an advertisement for a lawn mower race. Uncle Morty just couldn't pass that up. He returned to the farm and began modifying his big Toro lawn mower into a mean, competitive lawn-mowing machine.

But Uncle Morty also had other responsibilities now.

Soon after their last adventure—involving the president of the United States—Uncle Morty was given the Virtual Reality machine by the president. "Get this thing out of here," the president had ordered. Then, pointing an authoritative finger at Morty, he'd said, "You take it. We'll give you some money, and you can do research with it." Then he pointed that same finger at Terry Baker, his aide. "Ship it to his home. And be quick. I never want to see it again."

The president's experience with VR had been a little rocky.

Now Uncle Morty had not only the machine but money to upgrade his computer room and operate it exactly the way he wanted.

But he also had a contract with Terry Baker. Each month he had to show progress in his research by writing a report for Baker on what he had done. Writing a dull report couldn't hold a candle to lawn mower races. So, when Tim and Kelly expressed interest in working with the VR machine when he wasn't using it, Uncle Morty had quickly agreed. Yet he knew he had to get some final programming done before he could write the report, and he had to write the report today. Thus the alarm. When it went off, one of them was to get him.

Tim resented being forced to leave VR. He was just getting ready to race his Harley. And he knew he would beat Kelly—he had programmed it so she didn't have a chance. Now Uncle Morty was yanking him back to a world of heat and bugs—where he had to work.

"Maybe you could go get him," Tim called to Kelly.

"No—please? I drove your motorcycles—now I want to see what I programmed."

"Getting him will only take a minute."

"It never takes a minute."

Tim sighed and reluctantly pressed his palm escape button, leaving Kelly inside. His bike's roar faded as the visor went black. Then the visor rose as the zipper unlocked. He unzipped the suit and climbed out. For just an instant he watched his sister as she rode her invisible motorcycle. She made a turn, probably heading off to her own dream world. He hadn't talked to her much about it, having been busy programming his own. Now, no matter what she'd programmed, he was a little envious. She went onward while he had to leave.

Oh, well, he'd talk to her later that afternoon while they did the milking.

Something drew his attention away from Kelly—the tortured whine of Uncle Morty's lawn mower.

A moment later Tim stood on the screened front porch watching.

Uncle Morty sat on the tractor style seat and bounced and wavered as the lawn mower screamed over the broad front lawn.

Uncle Morty usually used his holstein cow, Elvira, as his official lawn mower. He would let her into the front yard on Saturday morning, and Elvira would work her way, a mouthful at a time, until she ended up on the opposite corner chewing her cud and pondering great thoughts. Of course, she wasn't a professional lawn mower. Sometimes she didn't eat evenly. On hot Saturdays, she'd spend most of her time beneath the sprawling weeping willow in the northeast corner near the road. Since last Saturday had been exceptionally hot, the grass was uneven, long and tangled everywhere but beneath the tree, where it was nice and short.

Wearing goggles and a Snoopy scarf, Uncle Morty fought heroically with the long grass, the engine giving its last ounce of commitment. Bent forward, eyes firmly riveted ahead, looking much like Tim thought he himself might look on his virtual motorcycle, Morty appeared as committed as the mower. He had to be to stay ahead. The tangled grass caused the mower to move in fits and starts until it broke through the tall grass to Elvira's short grass under the tree. No longer restrained, the Toro took off so fast that it slipped out from under Uncle Morty and left his behind planted on the newly mown, green grass. The Toro's throttle stuck and the machine roared on, slamming against the tree. One wheel in the air, the rotary blade chopped at the tree until the motor finally stopped.

Tim could only shake his head. Sometimes Uncle Morty was too strange.

Still sitting on the ground, Uncle Morty saw Tim. He laughed. "I suppose putting a jet engine on it might be overkill. Whadayathink?"

◉

Kelly saw the entrance to her dream world approaching. It lay at the end of a rainbow.

A nice touch, she complimented herself.

She had actually seen a rainbow once. She'd taken her father's lunch out to the field one day when he knew rain was on the way and couldn't spare the time to come to the house. The rainbow had arced from the clouds to the ground maybe a half mile off. Where it actually touched the ground they saw lovely, delicate colors—colors that seemed to grow more golden as they came to earth, like the pot of gold. She and her father had shared the magical moment.

These days Kelly was giving the computer more of her attention and less to the farm and even less to her dad. The VR rainbow brought a momentary pang of guilt as she realized that, but she didn't have time to think about that now.

She was anxious to see if what she had programmed really worked. And if it did, what it would be like.

She eased the motorcycle off the road onto a grassy path toward the end of the rainbow. Riding over a meadow, she pulled the bike to a stop at the rainbow's sparkling, golden edge. She dismounted and stood still for a moment. Her heart began to beat a little harder. Would it work? What if it didn't—was there danger?

She stepped into the colors, and the instant she reached the center of the rainbow the world around her, image for image, color for color, was replaced by another world—the one she had created.

It was a world of stone castles and armor-plated knights, of forests and lush, emerald grass. Kelly was on horseback—a beautiful Arabian. She had always wanted an Arabian—they were so powerful and noble. Her dad always had quarter horses on the farm because they were quick workers. This Arabian was midnight black, and it stepped with the air of a prince. Which was appropriate, for it carried a princess—Princess Kelly. Wearing an elaborate, sky blue, velvet costume right out of Robin Hood, Kelly rode from her father's castle and clattered over the lowered drawbridge into the surrounding meadow.

"Where are you going?" her virtual, bewhiskered father, the king, called down from the tall turret.

"Just to ride around the meadow," she called back. "I want to test my new invention."

"Another brilliant invention? You are such a wonder, my daughter."

"If it works the way I expect it to, you'll be able to earn enough money to build an addition to the castle. A game room, perhaps."

She heard the king laugh heartily and encouragingly. But when the laughter died his voice became grave. "The Crimson Knight is roaming around out there somewhere. He has vowed vengeance against you for burning his castle to the ground."

"But it was an accident," Princess Kelly called back. "I was merely testing my lightning machine—it was just one of those 'oops' kind of things."

"You fried his favorite cow."

"We replaced it."

"He's still angry—a knight's cow is sacred. The Crimson Knight can be vicious. Be careful. I couldn't stand for you to suffer like so many others have."

"Suffer?"

"We'll talk about it later, dear. I don't want to alarm you."

Princess Kelly only nodded. Nervously she looked about the meadow and into the surrounding forest, the emerald shadows dark. Someone could be in there watching her right now, and she'd never know it.

"I'll send out Sir Edwin."

"Okay," she said, glad that the king was taking the precaution.

Not far from the drawbridge stood an ancient oak. Kelly loved the shape of it. She had only told the computer that she wanted an oak there, and it had created a huge, wonderfully twisted tree, its lower limbs thick and reaching out in several directions.

The tree would make a good test.

From a leather sheath tied to her saddle she took out a device that looked like a television remote. Pointing the business end at the tree, she pressed the button and said, "Merry-go-round."

It was a curious transformation.

In a single fluid motion, the limbs drew in and the trunk began to spin, as did the limbs. The leaves and branches came together and became forms—horses, benches, big fish, all on poles, all rising and falling. Slowly music rose above the sound of breezes and filled the meadow.

A merry-go-round.

Now that was fun!

Kelly loved merry-go-rounds, and here in VR, with none of her friends watching, she could enjoy riding this one. She and her dad used to ride the one at the county fair when she was younger—they used to have a great time.

She slid down from the Arabian black and ran to the merry-go-round. Leaping onto one of the horses, she rode it around once then dismounted and walked back to the Arabian.

Sir Edwin, a bearded knight dressed in chain mail, had been watching from the base of the drawbridge and now galloped toward Princess Kelly. "How'd you do that? What is that thing? Music's pretty, but you won't go far on those horses."

"It's called a merry-go-round. It's a ride."

"A what?"

"Rides haven't been invented yet."

Sir Edwin shook his head. "For good reason. If I wanted to go around in a circle I wouldn't need that. But how did you do it?"

"With this," Princess Kelly said. She held up her device.

"Can it do something else?"

"Point at something."

Sir Edwin looked around. On the other end of the meadow stood a tall wooden tower. "Turn that into something."

Princess Kelly took a few steps toward the tower and pondered the possibilities. A thought struck.

"I need to be closer," she said, mounting her black.

The two of them trotted to within twenty yards of the tower and stopped. "Have you ever heard of a parachute?"

"Para-what?"

"Just watch."

Eyes narrowing more for effect than anything else, Kelly

pointed the device toward the tower. "Parachute ride," she declared.

The transformation was like the first one. The tower quickly turned from wood to metal. Iron arms grew out from the top, then billowing parachutes with two-person gondolas hanging from each one. Guide wires, three per parachute, dropped to the ground. When it was all done, the parachutes billowed as they descended.

"Want to ride it?" Princess Kelly asked Sir Edwin.

"Go up there? I'd fall. I'm a chubby knight."

Princess Kelly laughed as she placed the device in her dress pocket.

Sir Edwin was so chubby that his armor was specially made to encompass his large middle.

"I've always wanted to try the parachute ride," said Princess Kelly. "To see if I could do it. Come on, let's have a first try together."

"But, Your Highness, a knight must always keep his feet on the ground—or no further than horse-high from it."

"Where is that written?"

"In Proverbs, I think."

Princess Kelly chuckled and slid from her mount. "You're not afraid?"

"Certainly not, milady—well, just a little."

"Well," said Kelly, "if there's one thing I've learned it is to confront my fears."

The knight looked down at her for a long moment, then nodded. "Okay, I shall."

He swung his leg down, and after standing by the horse for a moment rethinking his decision, he stepped up to her. Together they walked up to one of the parachute gondolas.

"Well, milady, shall we?"

Swinging open the gate, they got aboard. "So we—" but Sir Edwin wasn't able to finish his sentence. The gondola jerked, then rose. Instantly Princess Kelly's stomach knotted. She knew she was afraid of flying. She also knew this wasn't flying. This was just rising, then gently dropping. But it didn't seem to matter. The moment the gondola left the ground, Kelly wilted into the corner.

"Milady, you're green."

"Green?" she said weakly.

"I find this rather interesting. Don't you?"

"I can't look," she groaned. They were about halfway up. "Please hold my hand, Sir Edwin."

"Your hand, milady?" Sir Edwin said. "But it's improper."

"Hold my hand!"

Sir Edwin grabbed it obediently and held it tightly.

The gondola stopped. They were cradled for a moment at the highest point—then they dropped. Kelly's stomach lodged in her throat. The part of her throat that remained unclogged screamed. "I'm falling—I'm falling—falling!"

"Yes, milady."

"Why did I do this—why?"

"You're facing your fears, milady."

When they were halfway down, Kelly completely lost it and wrapped her arms around Sir Edwin's biceps.

"I hope the king isn't watching," said Sir Edwin.

They were both quite relieved when the parachute came to rest on solid ground. By this time, Kelly had nearly dropped to her knees. Sir Edwin leaned over to help her to her feet. "Are you all right, milady?"

"She's fine," came another man's voice.

A hand in a crimson glove pulled the gondola gate open.

Both Kelly and Sir Edwin knew instantly the trouble they were in. They were staring into the fiery red eyes of the Crimson Knight!

Uncle Morty stared at the one occupied VR suit and the four others that hung on the wall.

Tim stood beside him. "If you don't want to go in, maybe I could. Maybe I could do the research and write the reports," he suggested.

Uncle Morty glanced at him then back at Kelly's suit. She looked like she was riding an invisible horse—riding it hard. "They paid *me*," he pointed out.

"But I'm the one who wants to do things."

Uncle Morty only nodded.

Tim knew what he was thinking: *I'm the genius. I'm the one who will make the breakthroughs, not you.*

Actually, Uncle Morty was thinking no such thing. He just didn't want to get into that black suit. "I hoped when I retired and came to the farm that I'd never have to meet another deadline." The phone rang and Uncle Morty answered it, thankful for even a momentary reprieve. But before he spoke into the receiver, he said to Tim, "Better signal Kelly to get out. I have to work alone in there."

Tim nodded and walked over to Kelly's VR suit and patted her hard on the back. As Uncle Morty answered the phone, he saw her press her palm button. Her visor rose. She looked unhappy. "You couldn't wait another few minutes? Things were really getting good."

"Uncle Morty needs the machine for a while."

Kelly unzipped the suit and stepped out of it. Tim unlashed it from the pedestal and carried it to where the other suits were hanging.

"You guys need to get home," Uncle Morty said. "Your dad sounds upset."

"Probably because I'm supposed to help Mom do some canning," Kelly told him.

"I'm sure I've forgotten something I was supposed to do too," Tim grumbled.

回

For the next couple of hours Tim stacked hay in the hay barn, the chore that Kelly had started that morning. There really wasn't much to do, but the intense heat in the barn made it a dirty, sweaty job.

Kelly's job was also hot. Her mother, June, asked her to boil the canning jars, then fill and seal them. Kelly worked for nearly two hours, then joined Tim as he finally rested on the bench swing near the duck pond in back of the house.

As she sat beside him, letting the swing move on its own, she said, "Pastor Cliff called. There's a youth group meeting tonight at seven. He's got a new project for us."

Tim nodded. "You going?"

"Don't know," she said, leaning toward him. "How's your program coming?" she asked, her voice noticeably more excited.

"I haven't gotten very far," Tim said. "But so far it's working okay."

"Isn't it great in there? To actually see and do the things we programmed."

"It's more than great. Even though you know what's going to happen, actually seeing it and walking through it—it's all new."

"Sometimes I forget that I've programmed something," Kelly said, "and when it shows up, I'm surprised. I want to go back to VR tonight."

"What about the meeting?" Tim asked.

Kelly shrugged. "What's your program do?"

"I'll show you sometime. What about yours?"

"You'll never see it. It's too good. I don't want you stealing it."

Tim laughed. "You're a ballerina again?"

"Remember when we were trying to get Dad to break away from the farm for a little vacation when we got back from Washington?"

"You just wanted see if you could get Gar to meet you someplace."

Gar Harkin was the son of the president of the United States. He and Kelly had met briefly during their last real adventure in VR. Kelly and Tim had saved him from serious injury—maybe saved his life.

"I bet I could have pulled it off. But, anyway, it's got something to do with one of the places we talked about."

"You programmed Disney World?"

"No." Kelly didn't laugh—he was right. "But I'm coming to the best part. Even though I know what's going to happen, I can hardly wait to see it. When will Uncle Morty be done?"

"Probably after milking." Tim paused for a moment, a new thought taking root. "You know, we're getting to be pretty good programmers. They need good programmers out there."

"Out where?"

"In the big world—Madison, Milwaukee, Chicago."

"You mean where there's no cows."

"Exactly." Tim pushed the ground to move the swing. "It's our ticket out of here."

"I'm thirteen and you're fourteen—any tickets we get now will expire by the time we're looking for jobs."

Tim glanced at his watch. "Time for milking."

Although it was seven-thirty in the real world, although the sun was slowly dropping toward the western horizon, it was only noon with a bright spring sun in Tim's world.

While Kelly did her thing in some other area of VR, he eased the Harley down the main road. A few minutes later the sound of the engine thundered off the trees, rippling off the lake. He turned from the main road onto a smaller one.

Before mounting the powerful black machine, he had taken a little time to program a few more features. He thundered through one of them now—a redwood forest. He'd seen it in one of his dad's travel magazines. His dad never traveled; he only read the magazines. After digitizing the picture, Tim let the computer expand on the scene, and within minutes he was ready to roar through the tall trees with the gnarled red bark and long, cool shadows.

He headed uphill, the engine screaming, his body leaning

forward over the gas tank. It was a position he liked. He felt in control, felt the power beneath him. He could do anything and go anywhere on this bike.

The forest ended. The trees gave way to desert—a broad, flat table of brown and reddish land.

He knew what was coming.

Another addition he'd just made.

He gunned the engine and felt the bike surge forward.

It was coming up. Any second. Just beyond that pile of boulders a hundred yards ahead.

His heart pounded with excitement, and he felt himself grin. There it was.

Opening before him, rainbow on rainbow of rock—the Grand Canyon. It was as if the earth had yawned, creating steep, tiered walls, some punctuated by green shrubs, others sheer and rugged—the Colorado River far below cutting through it. From this height it looked like a gentle ribbon of blue. Below, it tore savagely through the rock.

Tim gunned the engine again. Any second now he would reach the edge, and he had no intention of stopping. He glanced at the small dashboard. Next to the speedometer was a button. Tim poised his thumb over it.

The edge of the canyon came up fast.

His thumb rested on the button. He would have to push it at just the right moment.

A second or two now.

"Tim." He made it out as only a hint of sound above the Harley's roar. "Tim, over here."

Had he heard something? He wasn't sure. But there wasn't time to think about it. As he passed a pile of boulders, he pressed the button just as his front tire left solid ground, igniting the jets on the rear of the bike. "Whoa!" he cried, savoring the sensation of being carried off into space, above the gaping hole sprawling below him.

He *had* heard his name. The further the jets carried him, the more he certainly realized it.

And he had seen someone. Now that excitement was giving way to awe, he remembered. Perched on the rocks, just where he'd taken flight, was the very fetching, very fourteen-year-old, Sonya.

Sonya!

Was she really sitting on the pile of boulders as he roared by on the motorcycle? Although he truly wanted to know, he couldn't do anything about it now. He turned to see behind him. But he couldn't see anything—not because Sonya wasn't there, but because the further he turned the more unstable the flying Harley became. When it began to fishtail, he decided to straighten up.

Had she really been there? And why would she show up in something he had programmed?

Maybe it wasn't her. Maybe his imagination was getting the best of him.

A duck flew a few feet away from him, and as he glanced at it the jets propelling him sputtered.

Sputtered!

They can't be sputtering. That meant they were running out of fuel, right? They couldn't be—he had half a Grand Canyon to go yet.

He thought back.

He had pulled the jets out of a standard set of preprogrammed items. Jets were jets, right? He hadn't designated fuel capacity. Maybe he was supposed to do that. Maybe in the characteristics.

The jets stopped for nearly a second—the only sound was the rush of air at least a thousand feet above a valley of stone and a churning river. Then they fired up again. Tim heaved a sigh of relief. But the relief lasted only a heartbeat. The jets died again and this time remained dead.

On its own the Harley-Davidson motorcycle flies much like an anchor. Without the jets' persistent thrust, the bike's nose dropped, and following it came everything else—including Tim.

Uncle Morty sat at his Macintosh Power/PC writing his report. He hated writing reports, and he struggled over each word. His objective was to tell the truth without letting on that he had really done very little with the VR machine. He was having trouble.

So much trouble that he paid no attention to Tim's and Kelly's activities in Virtual Reality.

Princess Kelly returned to exactly where she had been when she'd pushed her palm button. Sir Edwin, at the point of a sword, was being ushered off into the surrounding forest. The sword was being held by one of the Crimson Knight's soldiers.

Another of the knight's soldiers grabbed Kelly and threw her onto her Arabian black, then led it quickly into the forest behind Sir Edwin.

As the shadows closed around her, she heard the king shouting from the castle turret. She couldn't tell exactly what he was saying, but he was definitely alarmed.

"Where are you taking me?" Kelly called to the Crimson Knight. Dressed completely in red, he rode up ahead of them, his red plume bobbing.

"You and your silly inventions have destroyed all I have," the Crimson Knight called back. "Now it's my turn to take everything of yours—including your life."

"Harm one hair on her head, and you'll have me to deal with," Sir Edwin warned.

"Ah, a threat—certainly it frightens me," the Crimson Knight mocked.

"I was a knight when you were in swaddling clothes," stated Sir Edwin.

"Precisely my point," the Crimson Knight said. "Now both of you be quiet. We have a ways to go, and I don't want to listen to you on the way."

Casually Princess Kelly felt in the pocket of her dress where she had placed her new device. It was still there. But how could she use it? Turning a tree into a roller coaster wouldn't do much to save her.

"My liege," came a cry from the back, "the king and his troops are approaching."

The Crimson Knight reined his red-draped horse and pulled around. "Is the trap set?"

"Trap?" Princess Kelly exclaimed. "What trap?"

"Spring it," the knight ordered.

That instant, the soldiers turned and disappeared back into the forest. Two remained—one pulling Kelly's horse and one with the sword in Sir Edwin's back. The Crimson Knight again took his place at the front, and the smaller group continued on.

A moment later they heard an eruption of cries and shouts from somewhere behind them. Then the clatter of swords, the *thwang* of bow strings. More cries—screams of pain.

Were any of them the king? Princess Kelly turned to see the

battle through the forest shadows. But it was too far off, and trees and shadows hid it from her.

"Keep going," the knight ordered.

"If you hurt the king—"

"You don't have to worry about the king anymore—and whatever happens to him is your fault. You and your inventions."

The battle raged. The cries, the *thwangs*, the roar.

"You used lightning—I will too."

"Lightning?" Princess Kelly said. Her heart began to moan inside her. It was her fault—if she hadn't been so creative the king wouldn't be fighting for his life right now.

"It won't be much farther," the Crimson Knight called back to them. "Then we'll really light up your life."

⊡

Uncle Morty was saved from his report by the phone. It was his brother, John, again.

"Sure," Uncle Morty replied. "They're both here."

"Doing what?" John Craft asked.

"Wandering around Virtual Reality."

"It's late. They've got to get up early for milking."

"I'll get them. Anything to stop working on this report."

John Craft hesitated. "Is all this Virtual Reality stuff healthy for good Christian kids?"

Morty took a moment to consider. "They're being creative," he offered. "Creative's good. God's creative—very creative. Programming takes discipline—there's only one way to do things, and if you don't do it that way it doesn't work. Discipline's good."

"What about running away from reality? What about missing a youth group meeting because of it? What about that?"

Uncle Morty leaned back in his chair. "Escaping from reality is like God giving us a coffee break. We all need one now and then. About the youth group? I've missed a few meetings in my time—we all have. It's the long haul that matters."

"The farm is their reality," John Craft argued. "They have chores, things that keep the farm running. Plus church things and people things. All *real* things."

"The novelty will wear off. When the new stuff takes work they'll slow down. Why don't you give 'em a few minutes more."

Uncle Morty heard his brother sigh over the phone. "A half hour," John said. "No more."

◎

They broke from the forest into a meadow. The Crimson Knight pulled up beside the princess. "We're going up there," he said and pointed to a tall hill at the far end of the clearing. "Wonderful," he said excitedly as he looked at the sky. "Storm clouds are gathering."

Kelly looked up. Clouds were beginning to come together, their black underbellies swelling with water.

"What's up there?" she asked, her voice weak.

"Your destiny."

"You can't do this," Sir Edwin protested. A stern poke in the back with a sword silenced him.

No more than ten minutes later they all stood at the foot of the hill. It rose abruptly from the meadow floor and looked as though someone had constructed it by piling up hundreds of rocks, then covering them with a layer of soil. Over the years, rain had washed away some of the dirt, exposing the rocks. But it wasn't the hill itself that drew Princess Kelly's attention; it was the single tree at its summit, a dead gray one with two shattered limbs reaching up as if pleading with heaven.

"You can't do this," Sir Edwin protested again. "She is a princess." This time when the sword poked him, he turned against it and was quickly struck by his captor. Although the chain mail on his shoulder prevented the blade from cutting him, he was driven to his knees.

"No, Sir Edwin," Kelly said, "it's all right. Jesus is in here with us." Kelly felt noble saying it. She had worked hard to include Jesus somewhere.

The name of Jesus wasn't lost on the Crimson Knight. He spat out the Savior's name. "It's got nothing to do with Jesus—it's got to do with trees on high ground during lightning storms. That's what it has to do with." Then he pulled his red-draped horse around and faced them. Indicating the soldier who held Kelly's reins, he said, "Take her up and tie her to the tree."

"Please, O Great Crimson Warrior," Sir Edwin said from his kneeling position. "Please reconsider."

But there was no reconsideration. The soldier holding Princess Kelly's horse let the reins drop. He grabbed her waist and pulled her off the mount. Then, without regard for her comfort, actually a little more roughly than she remembered programming it, he dragged her up the hill to the old dead tree.

Again more roughly than she thought she wanted, Princess Kelly was pressed with her back against the tree, and the soldier began wrapping a rope around her and the tree, securing her tightly to it.

By the time the final knot was tied, the Crimson Knight, the visor on his helmet up so that she could see his ugly, chiseled face, came up to her. He didn't say anything at first; he just turned and stared up at the clouds. The whole eastern horizon was black now, a billowing army with electrified artillery marching toward her.

Somewhere toward the horizon, a brittle shaft of lightning slashed from cloud to earth, the ground exploding at its electric touch.

The Crimson Knight remained silent, but when another distant flash of lightning broke free of the clouds and battered the ground, he turned toward Princess Kelly, pushed his ugly face an inch from her lovely one, and grinned.

Uncle Morty stood at the door to the computer room and watched Tim and Kelly in their black suits. The half hour had passed. What would he be interrupting? Tim looked like he was riding something, a bike maybe, turning the handlebars sharply back and forth as if negotiating a winding trail.

Kelly's black suit didn't move much. She just stood still. He wouldn't be interrupting anything there.

Stepping up to both black suits, he knocked them unceremoniously on their backs. Both of them required a second knock before they responded. Uncle Morty could tell there was some reluctance when each reached over to press the palm button. But before long the visors rose, and his niece and nephew stepped from their suits.

"You guys having a good time in there?" Uncle Morty asked while they hung up their suits with the others by the bookshelves on the wall.

"It's cool," Kelly said, the excitement she'd been experiencing still in her voice.

"Did Dad want us home?" Tim asked.

"You guys know you have to get up early," Uncle Morty answered.

"Maybe I could keep working on this all night," Tim said. "I could set an alarm, do the cows at five A.M., and then go to sleep."

"You're kidding," Kelly said. "Nothing's worth losing sleep over."

"Go home," Uncle Morty said wearily. "This'll be here when you come back."

Tim only nodded and glanced toward the machine as if saying good-bye to a friend.

There was nothing darker than the moonless country night they stepped into on their way home.

"Something's going on in there," Tim told Kelly.

"Always," she replied.

"I programmed my motorcycle to jump over the Grand Canyon."

"You little daredevil, you."

"But the jets ran out of fuel—"

"Jets?" Kelly sounded impressed. "You programmed jets?"

"I got them from the VR tool crib. That was the problem. I didn't know how much fuel they took or how long they burned. About halfway across they ran out, and I dropped like a rock. I was scared for a minute. I'd forgotten that I'd programmed it not to crash—"

"So the bike landed great, but you crashed?"

"The bike and I both landed on a ledge. But that's not the good part. I just drove along it. Sometimes the ledge was no more than a couple of inches wide, but the motorcycle never fell. Just as Uncle Morty knocked on my back I came to a cave—a big opening and pitch-black inside." Then he said with a strong edge of mystery, "I didn't program a cave." He went on. "I didn't program the lake we went by, either."

"The VR machine must create things for you," Kelly said. "It fills in the gaps."

"I used a brochure Dad had lying around to describe the canyon—I digitized a picture then entered its depth, length, width. I got some weather information from our encyclopedia, then some information about the river—it wasn't much. That's why when I actually saw it I was amazed at what the computer did with the little I told it. The cave was a surprise. I wonder if there're rattlers in there."

"You left snakes to chance? If it asks if you want snakes, I would say no, no, a thousand times no."

"I feel like sneaking back to Uncle Morty's tonight and going back in."

"You could. There're no locks around here," Kelly said. "Elvira came into his living room during the night once. He hadn't even closed the door. Do it, though, and you'll be so tired in the morning there's no telling what you'll attach to the milking machine."

"I wanna see what's in that cave."

"Probably just a few hundred bats—that computer makes bats really well."

After listening to a few stern words from their father about their responsibilities around the farm, the kids both headed up to bed.

Tim lay awake for at least another hour. He felt like an engineer at Disney World with an unlimited budget—and the imagination to spend it all.

He had another nagging thought. Had he actually seen Sonya in there? He didn't want to mention it to Kelly. She would only give him a hard time. But had he seen her? The impression was so fleeting that he couldn't be sure. At any rate, she was another reason to go back inside. Even if it wasn't her at the edge of the Grand Canyon, she might be somewhere else. Maybe the cave wasn't the most intriguing thing in VR.

Less than a mile away, secretive eyes watched Uncle Morty's house. Hidden behind the barn, watching for the lights to go black, stood a dark, shadowy figure. He'd been there an hour now, had seen the two kids leave—had even thought about following them. But there was no reason to. What he wanted was in the uncle's house.

Finally the windows went dark. After another half hour's wait just to make sure that Morty-guy was asleep, the dark form moved toward the porch and the front door.

CHAPTER 3

Hammond Helbert had escaped the Secret Service when they had discovered his computer laboratory in Maine by dashing quickly through a maze of tunnels that had quickly bogged down his pursuers. Using several disguises he then went to Washington, D.C., to keep an eye on the White House and the VR machine inside.

When the Burnham van backed up to the White House basement door and two large crates—probably the computer and digitizer—accompanied by several smaller crates were loaded into it, he knew *his* Virtual Reality machine was being transferred somewhere.

He was not surprised when he followed the van to Wisconsin and watched from a distance as the crates were unloaded at a very typical farmhouse. Nor was he surprised when he saw the Morty-guy and the kids. He laughed aloud at his good fortune.

For the next month he bided his time. He wasn't sure exactly how he would get his revenge, but he did know it would begin inside VR.

Now it was time to make his move. He would sneak in, accomplish his purpose undetected, then leave.

He heard snoring coming from the barn.

What was that? Maybe a tramp had found shelter for the night inside. Hammond stepped quietly to the barn door to identify the snorer. It was a beagle lying near the door on a bed of hay snoring contentedly.

Eager to get in and out before he accidentally woke the pup, he slipped quickly from the shadows across the parking area to the front porch. He was prepared to pick the lock, but he found the porch door unlocked. Without a sound he turned the knob and pushed it open. It squealed slightly—but only slightly—so he hastily squeezed through the opening. Finding the house door open as well, he entered. With the door shut behind him he froze and listened.

He immediately heard the telltale hum of the large computer. It came from a room not more than a few feet away. Taking a small penlight from his breast pocket, Hammond clicked it on and aimed the beam toward the room. There it was. *His* machine. If he thought he could have stolen it undetected, he would have backed a truck up to the house that instant. But there was no way he could take anything that big quickly enough. He knew beyond a doubt, though, that it would be his soon.

After taking another quick look around, he moved silently to the computer room. *A nice setup,* he thought, as he aimed the penlight in a broad sweep. But first things first. No matter what he decided to do, he would need to know what was going on in this room at all times. From his pants pocket he took a small transmitter. It was about the size of a dime with one sticky side. He stuck it to the bottom of a bookshelf beside the hooks upon which the black suits were hung. Then he grabbed one of the black suits and set it up on the wooden pedestal. After another look around, he climbed into the suit and secured himself, visor down, inside.

"Two Harleys," Hammond whispered, after his visor came alive. "At least they've got good taste."

In a distinct voice, he said, "Terminal."

Immediately a small device with a display and keyboard appeared in his hand. He quickly punched in an address and was transported to a circular room, the walls of which were covered with switches, identifying tags, and monitors—the VR control room. He quickly found the switch that would allow him to enter VR through a microwave hookup, as he had every time before.

He flipped it.

He was back in business!

Morty stirred. He'd gone to sleep easily but had awakened several times already, and he had only been sleeping uninterrupted for about two hours. He was worried. As a Christian he knew that God was turning everything he did, no matter how "dumb," to his good. But he still worried. He could feel his freedom slipping away. Soon they'd be expressing disappointment that he wasn't working harder—the pressure would grow, and he would have more deadlines. He was certainly smart enough to do whatever they wanted done, but he wanted to decide how to channel that intelligence. Yet, he had made a commitment—one he should honor.

Easing from the bed, the floor cool against his bare feet, he decided to get a glass of milk downstairs. The house was so quiet in the country. No horns honking, no trucks exploding by. Only crickets and sometimes the haunting call of an owl disturbed the night.

Walking downstairs, Morty realized that even his precious silence had changed. Now there was the incessant hum of the computer and the rush of air conditioning. It kept the house a little cooler, but it was disturbing to hear all these sounds of civilization when people were so scarce.

In the computer room, unseen by Uncle Morty, the black suit with Hammond Helbert in it moved with calculated, quick movements.

Uncle Morty reached the living room and crossed to the kitchen. When he was halfway there, the visor on Helbert's black suit rose—he was finished.

Just as Morty opened the refrigerator, Hammond unzipped the suit. He noticed the splash of light from the kitchen beyond the living room.

"Uh-oh," Hammond muttered.

As bottles clanked in the kitchen, Hammond Helbert decided to conceal himself. Easing himself out of the suit, he left it on the wooden pedestal and pulled a Glock 9mm pistol from his jacket pocket. He didn't want to shoot the guy. That would be too easy—too quick. He wanted him to suffer. But, of course, he would if he had to.

He hid behind the computer.

He heard the refrigerator door close.

Peering around the computer, Hammond could see Morty standing with his back to him. He was looking out the front door, his head cocked slightly as if studying the stars.

Hammond caressed the trigger with his finger. Quick or not,

it would be fun to shoot this guy. But that wouldn't be smart. He would leave a body, and the body would warn the kids, killing his hope of revenge on them. So he waited. Finally, when the milk was drunk, he saw Morty return to the kitchen, place the glass in the sink, and go back upstairs. Helbert slipped the gun into his jacket pocket and stepped through the computer room door.

But he had only reached the center of the living room when he heard scratching and whimpering at the front door. The barn beagle!

A light snapped on at the top of the stairs.

"Argh!" Hammond groaned, too far into the living room to dart back. But he was near the sofa and he dropped behind it.

"What do you want, Oscar?" Morty sighed from the top of the stairs.

Helbert heard the dog yelp in recognition. Then he heard Morty staggering sleepily down to the living room.

The front door opened, then the porch door squealed. The porch door clicked shut and, as the front door was squealing shut, Hammond heard the patter of little feet accompanied by wide-mouthed, tongue-hanging panting. A second later Oscar poked his head around the sofa corner.

Eyes wide, tongue pulled back, Oscar pressed a slimy nose against Hammond's forehead. Satisfied that everything was as it looked—this *was* a man and he *was* lying behind the sofa—Oscar withdrew his nose. Then, as his way of saying welcome, *schlurp!* He dragged a slimier tongue from Hammond Helbert's chin to his nose, catching Hammond's upper lip and yanking that up with it.

Enough! raged Hammond, reaching for his gun. He'd do the dog first, then the Morty-guy for letting the dog live. But before he could drag the weapon out, he heard, "Oscar, come on. Stop playing around. I'm tired. I've got things to do in the morning."

Oscar glanced reluctantly toward his weary master. He obviously liked licking people lying behind the sofa.

"Come on up here where I can keep an eye on you."

Oscar whimpered but finally gave up. His little brown and white rump scooted around the sofa corner, and Hammond heard the two of them heading upstairs.

Pushing the Glock back to the bottom of his pocket, he heaved a sigh of relief and wiped dog spit off his face. When the light went off upstairs, he relaxed a bit. He heard Morty tell the pooch to stay and then, wearily, to stop drinking from the toilet.

That reminds me, Hammond thought, *I'm thirsty.* He'd been feeling thirsty for more than an hour, since standing by the barn. Now he was parched.

There was a muffled creak from Morty's bed as he crawled into it, then a long groan as he made himself comfortable— probably hard to do on such a warm night. Hammond felt himself sweat as the house went silent.

He licked his dry lips. There had to be something to drink in that refrigerator. After waiting a few minutes longer, he rose to his feet and stepped cautiously to the kitchen. Placing himself so that he'd block the light, he opened the door.

No beer! Nothing but milk, orange and grapefruit juices, and a large bottle of water.

Farmers!

He grabbed the carton of grapefruit juice, found a glass in a cupboard, and poured himself a drink.

Leaning against the counter, he relaxed for a second and took a sip. As it turned out, it was the only sip he got.

He heard quiet, stealthy footsteps on the porch stairs.

Hammond's eyes popped like an owl's. Drink in hand, he looked around. Someone else was coming, and there was no-where to hide. Behind the sofa was out—he'd have to cross in front of the door to get to it.

He froze—in plain sight in the corner of the kitchen—just as the front door whined opened.

A dark, shadowy figure stuck his head in and whispered, "Uncle Morty."

Silence replied.

The shadow waited for a moment then pushed the door open. One of the kids—the boy.

Helbert pressed a hand against his gun but remained still.

The shadow stole quietly into the living room then over to the stairs. He looked up but didn't climb them. The boy stood there for a while as if deciding what to do. Finally, he turned resolutely toward the computer room and crossed to it.

When the kid disappeared inside, Helbert took a deep, calming breath.

He had to get out of there. He really didn't want to shoot anyone—they probably still hanged people in little towns like this. *Maybe they just run you over with a tractor and bury you in pig slop.*

But now he was curious. Why was the kid slipping in here in the middle of the night? Maybe this was something he could use in his plan. Hammond snuck along the wall to where he could see the kid standing over the discarded black VR suit he had just used. Maybe he was asking himself why it wasn't hung up. He finally climbed into it and pulled it up. Donning the helmet and zipping the suit up, he lowered the visor.

He's in. He's walking—getting on a bike or something—one of the motorcycles. He's riding it. This kid probably has to get up early in the morning to feed cows and chickens. Why is he sneaking around in Virtual Reality at, what? Midnight? The kid's hooked. Helbert laughed. Yeah, he could definitely use that.

◉

Every morning, Kelly and Tim worked as a team milking the cows. This morning was no exception. The routine was so set in their brains that they could do it in their sleep. Which was good because, after being up all night, Tim nearly was asleep. After running back from Uncle Morty's, he stumbled into the milk house, a sterile, cement-floored building adjacent to the barn. He found Kelly already there. She was just setting the stainless steel milk tank to "sanitation" and pushing the button. Instantly they heard a sound much like a dishwasher as a chlorine solution cleaned out the tank in preparation for the morning milk.

"Where have you been?"

"VR."

"All night? You snuck in Uncle Morty's house? What if he'd caught you?"

"He didn't."

"I can't believe you snuck into his house—a burglar—you're no better than a burglar. You won't be worth anything this morning."

"I'll be all right. I'll get some sleep later."

"Sure."

They both filled the troughs in the cow barn with ground feed, then they walked out to the paddock. Fifty cows waited for them. Some stood dull-eyed, others reclined—this morning, more so than other mornings, they all looked especially moronic to Tim. Clapping their hands, each closing in from an opposite side, Tim and Kelly jarred the cows to attention. They, too, knew the drill. Before long they began filing into the milk barn and into their respective stalls where they buried their noses in the troughs. One cow at a time, Tim and Kelly snapped the tie chains onto the cows' leather collars. The chains kept them comfortably in their stalls. At one time the Crafts had locked the cows' heads in place with stanchions made of galvanized pipe, but John Craft, always wanting the best for his animals, had torn out the uncomfortable stanchions a few years ago. While Kelly finished hooking up the chains, Tim started scraping the mud and manure from the walkway. *So far so good,* he thought, although his eyes ached and burned.

"You look like you're about to die," Kelly said as she snapped the last chain in place.

"I'm okay."

"You're nuts. And I bet you didn't even find anything out."

"I found out plenty."

"Yeah, right."

"You're just jealous because I'm more dedicated than you are," Tim said.

"The word is not dedicated—it's dead-headed."

Tim only sneered as he returned the scraper to its place among the other tools. Kelly went to the milk house and started piling the milking equipment: pipe, milkers, paper towels, pre-dip, and more on the pushcart. Tim helped her with the last of it, then pushed the laden cart back to the milking barn. Wordlessly, they laid the stainless steel pipe on the cement floor up to the glass collectors, then connected the food-grade rubber hose. A milker could handle two adjacent cows, and there were five milkers. Tim and Kelly could milk ten cows at once. When those were finished, they'd hook up ten more.

Hooking the cows up usually went slowly—this morning, with a headache waiting in the wings for Tim, he moved excruciatingly slowly. Working individually, he and Kelly dipped each cow teat in the pre-dip, a red, iodine-based solution that not only cleaned but bathed the tender skin in emollients to prevent chafing. After arduously drying the teat with paper towels, they hooked up the black rubber inflation to it and slid the stainless steel cup in place, four of them per cow. Tim's head was beginning to pound by the second cow. He hooked up two cows. Kelly did the others. Tim then fired up the milkers. As the combination of vacuum and electricity drove the pulsating milkers, Tim collapsed against a pipe stall.

"You sure you're going to make it?" Kelly asked, concerned.

"I need a Tylenol."

"You need eight hours' sleep."

While the milk flowed to the glass collectors in the milk house, then into the stainless steel milk tank where it would be cooled to just below fifty degrees, Kelly followed it. She liked to make sure all was working well. Tim usually did, too, but this morning he was happy just to be alive.

"Oh, no," she cried.

The valve at the base of the milk tank, the one used by the milk truck that collected the milk from the farmers, had been left open. The milk flowing from the cows was heading right down the drain. Kelly quickly grabbed the wrench-like handle and pulled it shut. The milk immediately stopped leaking and began filling the tank.

"How much do you think you lost?" came her father's voice.

Kelly straightened with a start. "Not much; we just started."

Her father only nodded. "We'll see how much is missing in the end. We've been getting about ten gallons per cow on average."

"I don't think it was much."

"Let's see how the rest of the job is going."

Kelly followed him into the milk barn.

Tim no longer leaned on a stall. He sat, head down, next to it.

"Tim!" his father's voice roared from the milk house door.

Tim shot up. Feeling dizzy, he grabbed the stall next to him. His head cleared—though it was still pounding—and he knew something was wrong. He also knew what.

"The valve was open, wasn't it?"

"Kelly closed it. The valve's your job. I made it your job so that you two would always know exactly who was responsible for it."

"I closed it," Kelly echoed, trying not to sound too self-righteous.

Tim hated it when he goofed up like this, particularly when it was clearly his fault.

"You okay?" his father asked.

"I didn't sleep well last night."

"Or at all," Kelly muttered under her breath.

John Craft only nodded and took a look around the milk barn. His eyes going about halfway, he stopped, craned his neck as if he'd seen something, and pointed. "You missed one."

Tim straightened and looked. Sure enough, the rubber inflations and tubes still hung from the hook on the stall piping. "You're each supposed to do half," his father stated.

"Oops," said Tim. "Kelly moved a little faster than I did. That's my fault too."

Missing a cow was serious. The cows needed to be milked twice a day or they could develop mastitis—swelling of the udder and fever. The antibiotics needed to cure them could make their milk unusable for up to two weeks.

Tim hurried to the cow's stall, flipped the milkers off, cleaned the teats, attached the apparatus, and flipped the machine on again. When the milk was flowing again, Tim remained by the cow he'd missed until his father finally left the barn.

The instant he was alone with Kelly again, his head dropped to his hands. "Now he'll be in here every morning to supervise us."

"Looks like you need it," Kelly said.

"Oh, go dry up someplace."

"If I did you'd probably kill these cows before long."

"Sure, right," Tim said sarcastically. "Well, no matter what happened, it was worth it."

"You couldn't have done anything worth Dad getting mad at us."

"The cave in VR was incredible," he told her.

The ten minutes it took for the first cows was up, and while they hooked up the next ten Tim told her everything.

"It reached far back into the canyon wall. It twisted and turned. Sometimes there were little waterfalls and places where the cave walls seemed encrusted with jewels."

"I want to see it."

"Fat chance. Anyway, after a while I came to a huge cathedral room. It had those stalactites and stalagmites. They were like teeth. I rode the Harley into this one, but I had to leave it there to go down the next passage. This one came to another big room. Like a ballroom. The lights were dim, but the walls were filled with colors. When Matthew Helbert designed the VR programs, he gave them an artist's touch."

"So it was just something cool to see? No action?"

"It was still something to see. It was great. And there are other caves leading off from those big rooms."

"I know what you're looking for in there."

"What?"

Kelly smiled knowingly. "Sonya."

"I am not." But it was obvious that he was lying.

"She's an old woman now. Why are you looking for her?"

"I'm not."

Kelly cocked her head disbelievingly. Then her eyes widened as if a bolt of understanding had struck her. "You changed her back, didn't you? When you stayed behind in the VR control room in Washington. You changed her back."

Tim hesitated, but then said, "I made her fourteen."

"So you *are* looking for her."

The cows hooked up, Tim flipped on the milker and leaned against a stall. "That's none of your business."

Kelly just snorted. "Not only is it none of my business, but I don't even care. I've got things I'm doing in there, and they beat your petty infatuation hands down."

Now it was Tim's turn to realize something. "You didn't call Sonya a cartoon—you didn't jab me. You've got a cartoon of your own."

"But mine's classy."

"Classy? A 'toon's a 'toon."

Kelly only smirked. "I'll stack my 'toon against yours any day you want. That is, if I can get back in there and actually find him."

"Let's get this milking done—maybe we can get back into VR this morning."

Feeling a sense of renewed energy, Tim started moving much faster.

Uncle Morty rose at about seven and was out in the front yard by eight. After feeding and milking Elvira, he did some weeding in the garden. Then he went to work on the lawn mower—he had the feeling he was nearing a speed break-through. He'd have that lawn mower flying before he was done.

While Uncle Morty worked, Hammond Helbert walked silently, purposefully, and secretly through Virtual Reality. Weeks before, in order to evade the army of Secret Service and FBI agents camped at his place in Maine, Hammond had used a specially prepared tunnel to extract the more important equipment from his lab. Moving only at night and using mostly back country roads, he had moved it all to a small, deserted farmhouse basement no more than a mile from Morty's farm. Once he had activated the high-speed telecommunications port in the Virtual Reality machine, he installed his line-of-sight microwave transmitter at the center of a dilapidated windmill and pointed it at Uncle Morty's house. He now used them all to enter into VR.

After about a half hour's investigation, he had browsed through what had been programmed in VR since his last frantic visit when he was in Maine. When he came to some interesting things those miserable kids had done, he made some changes. He didn't want to hurt them—not yet, anyway; if one was hurt the others might not go in again. But he did want the fun of scaring them a little. He would hurt them later—hurt them badly. That would be his revenge.

He formulated a plan—actually the skeleton of a plan. Somehow he would get all three of them into VR and keep them there—maybe turn off the palm buttons again and lock up the control room so they couldn't turn them on. Then he would punish them. They hadn't dismantled the electronics in the suits, so he could still hurt them badly. Just the thought of hurting them made him smile. It was a wonderful thought. They had beaten him twice now. No one did that—no one. Least of all two kids—and it was really the kids who had beaten him both times.

But there would be more than revenge. When this was all over, he would have that machine too.

CHAPTER 4

Tim and Kelly ate breakfast after milking the cows. As usual their father was out in the fields by then, having eaten earlier. June Craft greeted them as they pushed through the screen door. "Pancakes okay?" she asked.

"Sure," Kelly answered, sitting down at her usual place.

"Is any of Dad's coffee left?" Tim asked, poking around the coffeepot on the counter.

A little surprised, June nodded. "It might be a little cool. But you can use the microwave."

"You're gonna have coffee? Yuck," Kelly said.

"Where's the sugar?"

His mother found the sugar bowl and placed it on the counter. "You might want some cream."

Tim thought that was a good suggestion and combined equal amounts of coffee, sugar, and cream in a cup and placed it in the microwave for a minute.

"Your dad said you didn't sleep well."

"Worse than that," Kelly offered. "He's turning to a life of drugs right before our eyes."

Her mom placed a couple of pancakes on a plate and placed them before Kelly, then did the same for Tim.

Sitting down with the mug before him, Tim eyed the newspaper his father had left at his place. "Looks like your boyfriend got top billing," he said, pushing the paper over to Kelly.

On the front page was a picture of Gar Harkin. On an anti-gang speaking mission for his father, the president, he was touring some of the country's major cities. It was a story about his first stop in Miami Beach, Florida.

Kelly grabbed the paper and studied Gar's picture. "He's so good looking," she said.

"I still can't believe that you kids know people like that," June Craft said. "We met our congressman once, but only once. I can't even remember his name."

"Gar's the nicest guy. He gave me that rose. Remember the rose?"

"Yes, dear, I remember the rose."

"I'm pressing it in my Bible. Gosh, he looks handsome." Kelly sighed. She started reading the story while Tim poured syrup on his pancakes.

"Is he coming anywhere near here?" Tim asked. Actually he liked Gar too. The two of them shared an interest in computers—and both had visited VR. Tim had liked his visit, but Gar wasn't so sure about his.

"Chicago. That's pretty far from here," Kelly said.

"Too far for a day trip," their mother said.

"Maybe we could go to Chicago and meet him?" Kelly asked hopefully.

"We can't travel ten miles from the farm in summer," June said. "You know that."

Kelly eyed the paper disappointedly, then tossed it aside. "Someday there won't be a farm holding us back."

The words stung her mother, but she said nothing. "You guys want some eggs along with those pancakes?"

"No," said Kelly, a note of bitterness in her voice.

"Any milk?" Tim asked, frowning at his mug of coffee. "How can Dad drink this stuff?"

The phone rang. Kelly launched herself toward it, but Tim, being nearest, grabbed it. "Hello."

"Tim?" Tim recognized the youth pastor's voice. "Cliff Switch. How you doing? Missed you and Kelly at the youth group meeting last night."

"I had things to do."

"I'm sure. But we could use you. The fair's coming up in a month or so, and we're planning our booth. We're trying to make it an outreach. But a little more than just a place to hand out church brochures. You're always so creative—you and Kelly both."

"A booth at the fair?"

"Sure. The church would rent booth space, and for part of

the time the youth group would staff it. We want our time in it to be not only fun but God honoring—and a time to share the gospel. We're having another meeting tomorrow night to come up with ideas. I thought you two could be thinking about it in the meantime."

"Ideas for a booth? Sure, why not?"

"Good. So I'll see you both then. It'll be at the church about seven. Okay?"

"Sure. I'll tell Kelly."

"See you then."

Tim hung up.

"What was that all about?" Kelly asked.

Tim told her.

His mother nodded. "Good idea—Pastor Cliff's a good man. I'm glad we've got him."

"I don't think it's a good idea. I haven't got time for this," Tim protested.

"What else have you got beside your chores?" his mother asked.

"We're programming VR, Mom," Kelly told her.

"But this is important too."

"I guess," Tim said, the frustration in his voice evident.

"Go to the meeting tomorrow night. You'll have a great time. This kind of thing is right up your alley."

"I'm in a different alley now," Tim said, the lack of sleep making him irritable. Or maybe he just didn't like people demanding his time when he wanted to spend it somewhere else.

Tim and Kelly found Uncle Morty with the lawn mower again. He had already worn a racetrack around the barn and was determined to wear it even deeper. Elvira stood at the barn door watching, her large head moving from left to right as he passed her. She really wasn't sure what to make of all this.

"Uncle Morty," Tim called out.

Morty didn't slow down but waved.

"We're going into VR. Okay?"

Morty waved again.

Tim stood at the entrance to the virtual cave. Why did he feel so much at home here? Like he belonged? Like he knew it and it knew him?

He stepped into the dimly lighted opening. Even in the near darkness, the colors leaped from the cave walls—almost magic in their brilliance. Having been there before, he experienced a new confidence and began walking.

Soon he was making the same turns, finding the same domed rooms, the same stalactites and stalagmites. To his surprise, after only a half hour he began to get bored.

Maybe he should leave the cave and explore more of the canyon. *If there's one cave there will probably be others, or maybe something entirely different,* he thought. After all, this was Virtual Reality—there were probably virtually real things out there that the computer would find commonplace that he would find incredible.

"Tim."

A voice.

He now stood at the center of one of the large cathedral rooms. This one had a whole mouthful of 'tites and 'mites, as well as frothy pillars that had formed when the 'tites hanging from the roof met the 'mites building up from the floor. They all glowed translucent orange and brown.

When he heard the voice, though, he didn't care about any of that.

"Sonya?" he called out, the echo bouncing playfully from wall to wall to ceiling to floor.

"Tim?" she replied.

"Where are you?"

"You can't see me?"

"No. Where are—?"

"Look to your right—no left, it's my right—and up."

There she was, high on a ledge, standing fearlessly. But she didn't look like herself. She looked younger—no longer like a temptress. Now she was more pert and alive. *But that's the way she should look. She's fourteen—my age. A great choice,* he thought.

She was cute in her jeans and flowery blouse, with her auburn hair streaming down over her shoulders.

"You coming down?" he called.

"You come up. I want to show you something."

"Up there?"

"Scared?" She laughed.

"I'm no mountain goat," Tim said.

"And I am?"

"Well, no. Where's the path up?"

"Over there," she said, pointing toward a small break in the cathedral wall.

"See you in a minute."

Actually it took a little longer than that. The ledge was narrow, the steps from ledge to ledge tenuous. A couple of times rocks loosened and slipped from beneath his feet. He saved himself by grabbing other ledges and finding new places to stand. By the time he'd gone halfway, he'd decided that before he came back again he would program an elevator.

But he made it and finally stood before Sonya for the first time since returning from Washington, D.C.

Up close the difference in her years was even more pronounced. Before—when she was twenty-two—she'd had a certain allure. Her eyes were soft and fetching, her smile reached out and caressed his heart. Now her eyes smiled and danced with mischief, searching for fun.

"Hi," he greeted.

"I'm glad you got back all right," she said, relieved.

"You remember all that?"

"I remember everything. You ought to see my memory file. But who would want to do that, right?"

"It's good to see you," Tim told her, instantly aware of his self-consciousness. She was only a cartoon, but he felt the same discomfort that he felt when talking to a real girl.

"Me too."

"You said you wanted to show me something."

"Follow me." Sonya turned around. "It's over here."

The ledge they stood on was a foot or so wide, and the wall next to them arched in toward the dome. Sonya, who was just a little shorter than Tim, had to stoop slightly to move. But she only moved a few steps. Then she eased herself through a crack in the dome. It was barely wide enough for her and very tight for Tim, but he finally squeezed through. When he emerged on the other side, what he saw was eye-popping.

The new room glowed from a hidden source of light, maybe the walls themselves, and lighted a natural water park. The floor of the room was an immense pool that splashed from wall to rocky wall. Feeding it were waterfalls—big, surging ones, small trickling ones, and every size in between. They circled the pool as did boulders and ledges for diving and resting. From everywhere came the sound of rushing water, and everywhere the colors of it. Emerald greens and broad washes of blue and yellow, and reflections of light danced off the pool.

Tim's mouth dropped to his knees.

"Like it?" Sonya asked, her eyes sparkling as if she knew his answer already.

"It's wild. Like a water park or something."

"It's better than that," she laughed and began slipping off her tennis shoes.

Just below them, gushing from the wall, was a white, frothing waterfall. It spilled from the rock, reached out several feet, then plunged to white water below.

"What are you going to do?" Tim asked.

"Have some fun. Wanna?"

"You're going to jump—our clothes'll get wet," he said, forgetting for a moment that their clothes would only *seem* wet.

"They'll dry. So will you. Come on." Leaving her shoes where they landed, she leaped feetfirst off the narrow ledge onto the billowing water. The instant she hit the water, it carried her down into the pool beneath.

Tim didn't see her come to the surface.

Without hesitating he threw his shoes off and jumped. Less than a second later the frothing water hit him. As with Sonya, it carried him out and down. Driven below the surface, he felt the force of the waterfall keep him there until he swam from beneath it. He came to the surface, took a needed breath, and dog-paddled, looking in all directions for Sonya. She reclined on a nearby boulder as if sunning herself.

"You okay?" he called out.

"Sure. It's great, huh?"

"I thought you'd drown or something."

"Why would you think that? Come on. There's something even better over here."

Although excited, Tim was still feeling the effects of a night without sleep and didn't move as quickly as he might have. He struggled onto the rocks, then followed Sonya laboriously as she moved far more lithely than he up a pile of boulders to another waterfall. This one was narrower and gentler than the last and slid in rhythmic waves down a series of flat rocks—a water slide that ended about five feet above the water.

The instant Sonya reached the top she threw herself belly down and headfirst and slid like a seal down the rocks. When the slide ended, she was launched into the air. As if trying to fly, she spread her arms, floated for a few feet, then dove into the waiting pool. Smiling and pushing her hair out of the way, she resurfaced and called up to him, "I'll wait down here for you."

To Tim it looked like a long drop. But if Sonya could do it . . . He let himself down as gently as he could, feet and bottom down, and started to slide. This was fun. The water carried him along. When the slide ended, his speed tossed him out over the water. Then the pool engulfed him—the wet, the cool. The VR suit didn't simulate it all perfectly, but it was good enough to give him a genuine thrill.

This time, however, he swam beneath the water for a moment or two, feeling the buoyancy. A school of fish swam by. About goldfish-size, they moved as one in a large wedge. Seeing him, they reversed course, the whole school reflecting the available light in a metallic flash as they turned and sped away.

Coming to the surface beside Sonya, he splashed her then dog-paddled to stay afloat.

"There's fish in here," he told her.

"Who cares about fish?" Sonya chided. "I dare you to go down the slide headfirst."

"Yeah, right," Tim fired back.

"Come on. We'll go down side by side—holding hands."

"Holding—"

"Hands—right. It'll be fun."

"Is there enough room for both of us?"

"You calling me fat or something?"

"Fat? Never."

To launch themselves they stood on either side of the narrow waterfall holding hands over it. Her hand was soft and strong, and her touch sent a warm thrill surging through him.

You know I'm really a little nuts, Tim thought. *After all, she's only a computer character.*

"Okay, on three we both dive," she said. "Bend your knees like me."

He did.

"Okay, one, two—you ready? Three."

They both dove forward. Tim felt his belly slap the rocks, felt the waves lift him from the rocks and carry him down, saw the water lapping at his chin. He also felt Sonya's hand holding his tightly. He stole a glance at her. She was smiling expectantly at him—wondering if he was having the fun she was.

When the rocks ended they were propelled out over the water. Tim let go of her in order to dive, but she didn't let go of him. Holding his hand even tighter, she led him into the water, then stayed with him below it as they broke through another knot of fish, and still remained with him when they bobbed to the surface.

That's when she let him go. But for only a second. She wrapped her arms around his neck and while he paddled to keep both of them afloat, she grinned happily into his face. "Wanna do it again?"

"Can we just sit for a while? Maybe talk or something."

Sonya laughed. "Talk," she taunted, spinning away from him and giving him a couple of quick splashes.

He dodged, but didn't return them. "I'm not up to that. I'm tired. I didn't sleep last night." Without waiting for her, he swam to a nearby rock just beside the water slide. Easing himself out of the water, he leaned against another boulder.

Sonya splashed around in the water for a moment or two but then gave up and swam Tim's way. She joined him and leaned against the same boulder, pressing her shoulder to his.

"Okay, what do you want to talk about?"

"I hate conversations that start that way. I don't know what I want to talk about. . . . Okay, what have you been doing since I saw you last?"

"Waiting for you."

"How can a computer character wait for me?"

"I don't know all the technical things, but over time we computer characters gravitate toward people. It was an experiment Matthew tried and never changed. I've gravitated toward you. That's why I waited for you."

"So we're going steady?" Tim asked jokingly.

"Okay," she said.

Tim swallowed hard and changed the subject. "Did the computer create this place, or did I? If I did, I sure don't remember doing it."

"I don't know. But I knew where it was, and usually that's

because the computer creates it. Otherwise I would have just found it. It's fun, isn't it? The creator, Matthew, liked fun and beauty. That's what the computer usually creates."

"Like you."

Sonya, the computer character, blushed. "Are you sure you just want to sit here? We could go down the slide a few more times, or dive for treasure."

"Treasure?"

"Things on the bottom. I bet there are things on the bottom."

"So you don't know if there are."

"I bet there are."

"What things?"

"Surprise kinds of things. I bet they're there, and if they are it would be fun to dive for them."

Tim was almost tempted to test out her theory, but not quite. The lack of sleep was fast catching up to him. He had to close his eyes—just had to. Keeping them open was becoming too much of a chore.

"My eyes are burning, and I just want to rest them for a few minutes."

Sonya brought a consoling hand up to his shoulder and gave him a pat. "I never get tired. I don't think about that."

Tim smiled as a mist of relief broke over him. He closed his eyes.

When he opened them it was like awaking to a dream. Sonya's lap had somehow become his pillow, and she now smiled sweetly down at him, her fingers gently massaging his temples.

"You slept a while," she said softly.

"How long?" he asked, a little concerned. Though he had done all the incidental chores, there was always the afternoon milking, and he didn't dare miss that. Not after this morning, especially.

"An hour and twenty-two minutes."

Calculating in his head, he decided he was still okay—not by much, but okay. He still had a few minutes left.

No he didn't.

He felt a steady, hard knocking on his back. He hated being knocked on the back as if he were a door. When would he and Kelly go back to sending messages through the computer like they used to?

"I guess I have to go," he told Sonya.

"So soon? We could play here all day."

"I should get you some virtual cows so you'll understand why I can't."

"I'll miss you," she cooed.

"You don't know the meaning of the word like I know it."

"Sure I know the meaning of *miss*. The American Heritage Dictionary, the seventh meaning (the one most apropos) is: 'To discover the absence or loss of.'" She leaned down close to his lips. "You're going to be such a loss."

Tim's heart went to mush.

Slightly refreshed from his nap, he stood and was about to scoop her up and toss her into the water when the knocking came again—far more insistent this time. He sighed, then looked deeply into those incredible eyes, waved a sheepish good-bye, and pressed his palm button.

◉

Lurking close by, hidden by a protruding rock, was Hammond Helbert. He had followed Tim, and that Kelly-girl, too, throughout their VR journeys, sometimes behind them, sometimes ahead of them, bouncing around by inputting addresses into his little terminal. His plan was slowly coming together—piece by evil piece. He knew that if it was going to work this time he had to stay close and view things firsthand. Only by doing that would he gather enough information to assure success.

And he *was* going to succeed this time.

Now, as Tim disappeared, Hammond watched the lovely young girl—was that Sonya?—get to her feet, stand quietly for a moment, then evaporate into the mist. *Why isn't she the old hag I turned her into the last time? It doesn't matter. She brought the kid back, that's what matters.*

Hammond pushed off from the boulders and swam lazily for a while. In all his wanderings through Virtual Reality he'd never really enjoyed it. For him it wasn't something to enjoy; it was something to capitalize on, exploit, and make money from—a huge pile of money.

But now that he had eluded the Secret Service and the FBI, now that there was no one to follow in VR, now that his plan was beginning to come together, he took a moment to relax and swim.

His brother had done a remarkable job of simulating everything. It actually felt like he was swimming, like the water was buoying him, providing resistance as he stroked and kicked. It was relaxing and cool.

I wonder how the Kelly-girl is doing, Hammond mused as he swam. *I wonder how she's coping with those little changes I made to her program.* He laughed contentedly.

Something brushed against him. Then another something.

He stopped swimming, paddled for a minute, then pushed his face into the water. Fish. Hundreds of them—small, goldfish-sized, darting playfully in schools, dancing and flashing the reflected light as if choreographed. He wasn't one for finding things cute or endearing, so he only found them fascinating. One came up to his face, its mouth working, its eyes wide with curiosity. It stayed there an inch from his nose as if waiting for Hammond to do something entertaining.

Hammond brought his hand up and cupped the fish and studied it for a moment.

The last of his plan came into focus. He smiled at the little creature. Yes. That's what he'd do. He mouthed a single, horrible word: *piranha.*

CHAPTER 5

While Tim was going wild in the computer-generated water park, Kelly found herself tied to the tree at the top of the rocky hill, a lightning storm blowing in.

Now, with black clouds boiling overhead, the Crimson Knight stood facing the approaching storm, his back to her. She had to admit, he *was* a snappy dresser. His form-fitting armor was draped with a red cape. His red boots were the thickest leather, and his helmet was crowned by a fluffy red plume.

She was beginning to hate red.

Her attention was drawn away to the east. The blackness about a mile off ignited as lightning streaked from cloud to cloud.

"It won't be long now," the Crimson Knight said, rubbing his gloved hands deliciously together. "Fried princess."

"You can't do this!" cried Sir Edwin from down below. "She's done nothing."

The guy in red turned. "She burned down my estate. She broiled my cow. I loved that cow—milk, cheese, yogurt. Wonderful cow."

A ragged, fiery dart struck the far edge of the forest. As she thought about her dilemma, Kelly realized she was at the center of a giant dart board. That dart, thrown from cloud to ground, hit the very outside circle. But soon they would begin to hit smaller and smaller circles on their relentless march her way.

She felt a few drops of rain and heard a peal of thunder, dull with distance. More lightning, this a little closer—the next smaller circle on the board.

"Look," the red guy exclaimed, pointing off toward the surrounding forest. "A fire where it struck."

She peered over the knight's shoulder. A thick, gray column of smoke rose from the trees. A moment later fingers of flames erupted from the base of the column.

"That's what lightning does—that's what your lightning did. Why did you make such a thing?"

Kelly hadn't expected a question. When she programmed the conversation monitor, no questions were included. But there it was. The computer was making things up. "I made it because I could," she replied. "It just got away from me."

"You'll burn like that. A crack of thunder, a flash of electricity, and *Poof!* You'll be the 'poof' part." He laughed. But then he sighed sadly as the clouds opened up above the fire and doused the distant flames in a sudden downpour.

Could she escape? She was tied to the tree by a rope wrapped around her and the tree several times. Her hands were forced back behind her. Could she work them forward? If she could she might be able to get to her new invention—and turn the knight into bumper cars or something.

The rain came down a little harder now.

Another flash of lightning. Another tree exploded in the forest, the rain quickly overpowering the flames.

Near the edge of the meadow came a commotion. Voices calling and crying, men locked in combat—some in red, others in the king's forest green. They broke from the forest into the meadow, swords flashing, metal slapping metal.

The trap that the Crimson Knight had set must not have worked completely. The battle still raged, and now it spilled out into the meadow.

Princess Kelly cried down to them, "Is my father still alive?"

No one answered. The soldiers in green were too busy fighting for their lives.

She saw Sir Edwin come alive. He pushed aside the sword that held him captive. The soldier holding it spun and tried to bring the sword back down upon Sir Edwin, but an inspired Sir Edwin launched toward him and drove him back. The soldier stumbled as Sir Edwin drove him to the ground.

Kelly's attention was drawn away from the battle by another blast of lightning. The darts were falling into smaller and smaller circles. Now they had marched about halfway through the eastern forest that bordered the meadow. It wouldn't be long before they would be striking the hill itself.

Why did she choose lightning anyway? Why couldn't she have been threatened by the Pillsbury Doughboy or someone throwing marshmallows? When she was programming all this she remembered a story she had read once where the hero won the battle and his true love because of a God-sent lightning bolt. It had seemed like such a powerfully exciting thing from which to be saved. But now Kelly wasn't so sure. The computer was beginning to do its own thing, and one of those things could be to send one of those lightning bolts her way. And if the lightning did get too close, with her hands tied like they were, there would be no way to get to her palm escape button!

More cries from down below. It wasn't a large battle anymore. Not many soldiers were left on either side, but it was fierce. In the growing rain the swords flashed and clanked together. Kelly heard a horrific cry as one combatant ran through another.

The march of lightning toward her continued. This one blew the top off a tall tree. The blast was frighteningly loud.

The rain came down harder. The battle below blurred to gray. Men began slipping in the mud, swords slashed at air more often than at another soldier. As Princess Kelly studied the battle, she saw a ray of hope—from her vantage point on the hill, it looked like the green army was winning. Sir Edwin had taken his captor's sword and was wreaking havoc on the red army with it. He was so successful that most of the soldiers lying in the grass were red, while the green soldiers fought harder against the red ones who remained standing.

The Crimson Knight must have seen the same thing. As another lightning dart was hurled from boiling black clouds, he drew his sword. With red cape flying behind him, he leaped down the hill into the battle.

The instant he left her side, Kelly began feverishly working her hands forward trying to escape. But it wasn't going to be easy. Not only were the ropes tight, now they were heavy with the rain. Her wrists were quickly chafed. But she couldn't give up.

Blam! Lightning—a jagged flash slashed the air and slammed into a tree at the edge of the meadow. It exploded then erupted in flames, which were quickly doused by the rain. It happened so close to the battle below that for an instant everyone froze—but only for an instant. The battle quickly resumed, and Kelly started working her hands forward again, pushing them between the ropes and the tree's dead wood. But they hardly moved at all.

The Crimson Knight, his long sword swinging like a scythe, was having a devastating effect on the soldiers in green. Even though the rain turned him to a blur, his quick, decisive movements took him everywhere, and everywhere he went, a green-clad soldier fell.

Finally it was just the Crimson Knight and Sir Edwin. Sir Edwin turned from having dispatched the last of his enemies in surprise to see the soggy, red-plumed knight standing before him, his sword waving before Sir Edwin's chest in a wordless challenge.

Sir Edwin swallowed hard, nodded his acceptance, and brought up his sword. They touched steel edges as a ceremonial start to the battle, then faced off.

Due to his superior strength and skill, the Crimson Knight took an early advantage. Through quick jabs with his sword, he pushed Sir Edwin off balance. When Sir Edwin stumbled, the man in red slammed him again and again, the clanking muffled by the rain—but it was loud enough to draw Kelly's attention. She stopped her struggle for a moment, long enough to see the Crimson Knight standing over Sir Edwin, the point of his sword pressing against Sir Edwin's throat.

At that moment the sky split apart with a raging clap of thunder, then a jagged lance of lightning came down. It struck the base of the hill, sending a severe shock wave up the core of the hill to the tree, right up Kelly's spine.

The instant the lightning struck, the Crimson Knight straightened. When the earth stopped shaking, his sword still pressing against Sir Edwin's throat, he turned toward her and cried out, "Now. Prepare to fry!"

She was still reeling when she heard another voice from down below. It was an urgent, distraught voice—the king's. "What is he doing to you, child?" he cried.

Eyes wide, she cried, "You're alive!"

Not only was he alive, but he wasn't alone. Obviously picked up somewhere in the forest, the king rode on a horse behind the most magnificent knight she had ever seen—a Prince Charming. Dressed in white, this newcomer approached the battlefield with an overpowering aura of confidence.

"It's about time," Kelly muttered.

Another blast of thunder was followed by another bolt of lightning. It struck and tore a hole in the hill a little way from the base. The darts were closing in on the human bull's-eye. Again she shuddered.

The new knight reined in his horse in front of the Crimson Knight, then allowed Kelly's kingly father to dismount. When the king was on the ground and safely away from the fight to come, the White Knight looked up at Princess Kelly. Seeing her situation, he turned his attention back to his red enemy. He ordered in a clear, strong voice, "Let that soldier go and release the woman."

"He's not important, anyway," said the Crimson Knight, lifting his sword from Sir Edwin's throat. The instant the blade was lifted, Sir Edwin rolled aside. When he got to his feet he was quickly taken hostage by another red soldier.

Now the Crimson Knight waved the point of his sword in the White Knight's direction. "But you are important. Of course, if you come down here you might get your clothes dirty."

"It is not my clothing that will be soiled. It will be the point of my sword. Now, untie the woman."

There came another deep rumbling of thunder. Princess Kelly peered up into the black clouds just in time to see a fiery lance launched in her direction. It struck the hill as had the other two, but this one was just a little closer.

The Crimson Knight laughed. "The only way she will be untied is if I am no longer alive to prevent it."

"A sound plan," said the White Knight. "On horseback or on foot?"

"Will you two guys get on with it?" Kelly cried. "I don't have much time here."

As if to prove her right, another bolt of electricity hammered the hill. Like the last, this one sent an earthquake charging up her backbone. Unlike the last, it dislodged a boulder that rolled to the meadow, narrowly missing the two knights.

Watching the boulder roll to a stop, the White Knight called back to her, "You have a point, milady." He threw a leg over his horse's neck and slid deftly to the ground. An instant later his sword was unsheathed, and he faced his crimson foe.

Kelly was shocked. "A sword? You're not supposed to use a sword," she cried. The computer was changing things. Or had she programmed it wrong? She certainly hadn't given her White

Knight a mere sword, and with the lightning getting closer, an error could hurt—a lot.

Like Sir Edwin, the king was also a prisoner now. A red soldier pointed a sword at him, daring him to make a hostile move.

Neither the Crimson Knight nor the White Knight paid attention to any of this. Their swords at the ready, they stalked each other.

"You don't have time for this," Kelly cried. "Finish him off, and get me out of here."

But the White Knight remained calm. His armored visor was down, and Kelly hadn't yet seen his face, but from the slow, determined way he was moving, she knew it was expressionless.

The red guy attacked. Seeing an opening, he launched himself at his enemy swinging his sword repeatedly like an ax. The White Knight, though driven back, took the advance in stride, blocking each chop expertly. When it looked like he might actually be in trouble, he spun away from the onslaught and brought his sword down on the Crimson Knight's shoulder. Although the armor deflected the blow, it slapped the warrior off balance so that the White Knight could slam him again.

The Crimson Knight recovered quickly, though, spinning out of harm's way. When he replanted his red boots he faced the White Knight as before, ready for anything.

Although the White Knight had won the first encounter, Kelly was finding it hard to cheer. The instant they reset themselves for the next attack, another bolt of lightning crashed into the side of the hill. The point of impact being higher than the previous one, the shudder up her spine was far more intense, far more terrifying. These things were getting far too close. How would the black suit simulate a lightning strike? Just the thought of it made the hair on the back of her neck stand on end.

"Come on, down there," she cried. "Put the sword away and use the hammer."

The White Knight didn't seem to hear her. He had other things on his mind—the Crimson Knight's continued stalking for one.

Again the red guy attacked, again he slammed the White Knight's sword as if he were wielding an ax. Again the White Knight pulled back, but this time, instead of spinning out of the way, the White Knight fell backward. For an instant Kelly's heart stopped. The White Knight couldn't lose! That wasn't possible. She had written it—

Although she had been staring down the hill at the White Knight's plight, she suddenly caught sight of something going on above her—right above her. The black clouds were everywhere, it wasn't that. But now the clouds seemed to be gathering just above her head—black, boiling clouds; angry, violent clouds. It was as if they were gathering all that they had together so that they could dump it all on her at once.

Were they gathering for one last, colossal lightning strike? She hadn't written it that way, but she hadn't prevented it either. She had told the computer she wanted a storm, some lightning, and where she wanted the lightning to strike. The lightning was already striking closer than she wanted; maybe the computer was about to clobber her as well.

It also looked like the Crimson Knight was about to do some clobbering himself. The White Knight was on his back, and the red guy continued to lay into him. With his sword held above his head, the White Knight was holding him off, but only barely.

"I should have created King Kong—he would have just stepped on him," Kelly grumbled.

She looked up. The clouds were still gathering in a huge, inverted bubble. Something was going on up there.

Below, the Crimson Knight reared back to deal the death blow. He pulled his sword way back above his head, preparing to bring it down with all his might. Then he let fly. Before he made contact, though, the White Knight rolled and, with more agility than his armor would seem to permit, leaped to his feet. The sword he was carrying instantly changed to a huge mallet. It was a massive mallet—a Wile E. Coyote mallet.

The Crimson Knight shrank back from it but to no avail. The White Knight brought it down with great precision—right on the top of the red guy's plume. Since the ground was wet from the rain and the knight's armor made him quite rigid, the blow drove him into the ground—Wham! Wham! Two strikes and he was buried up to his chest.

The red guy no longer a threat, the White Knight tossed the mallet aside and turned his attention to Kelly.

None too soon, Kelly thought.

With the Crimson Knight out of service, the red soldiers

holding Sir Edwin and the king fled into the forest, after releasing their prisoners.

The gathering clouds had stopped gathering. The bubble directly above her head had stopped growing and was now drawing within itself as if preparing to spit something at her. She had never seen clouds behave this way, but then she'd never been tied to a virtual tree in a virtual storm waiting to be fried before.

"Get up here, quick!" she cried.

But the White Knight had already launched himself up the rain-soaked hill, his boots digging deeply into the wet earth, gaining footholds on exposed rocks, his hands scrambling to assist him. Within seconds he reached her.

"Oh, praise God. Now get me out of here."

The White Knight grabbed a small dagger from his waist, sliced the ropes with a quick stroke, pulled her away from the tree, then dove with her down the side of the hill.

An instant later the cloud spit what it was preparing to spit—an immense white charge of electricity leaped down to the tree. The tree burst into flames, and it splintered from tip to root. Smoldering pieces of it fell around Princess Kelly and the White Knight, safely in the meadow below.

"Are you all right, milady?" the White Knight, her brave Prince Charming, asked. He had landed in the mud near her. Now he quickly jumped to his feet and extended a helping hand.

She took it, and when she did, he lifted his visor. He was as wonderfully handsome as she had hoped, and the strong touch of his hand brought with it a warm sense that all was well.

The king and Sir Edwin also crowded around her, the king weeping tears of joy.

Why wasn't it enough for her?

And what happened to this computer anyway? That was just too close. Even for a Prince Charming.

While these thoughts were charging through her mind, she felt someone patting her insistently on her back. "I wonder when we're going to get back to sending messages," she said to herself. "At least I could ignore those for a minute."

She turned to Prince Charming's deep blue eyes and chiseled cheekbones. "I have to go."

"I shall miss you, milady. My heart is a slave to beauty and purity. My heart is a slave to you, for you are the very fount of both."

Kelly smiled. "That's nice—very good—yes—very, very good."

She pressed her palm button.

🔲

Hammond Helbert arrived several minutes after Kelly left. Mild curiosity brought him. He had seen the results of Tim's programming, and he liked what he saw. He could easily use it as part of his plan for vengeance. He had seen the Kelly-girl's programming, but not what the programming produced. Now he stood at the edge of the meadow. The Crimson Knight was still buried to his chest, and the White Knight nursed two old soldier's wounds, but it was what remained of the tree that captured his imagination. It was a hollow tangle of smoldering splinters. Had she still been tied to it when the lightning hit, she now would be in the hospital. It was simulations like these that brought a strong dose of reality—and electricity.

Hammond Helbert laughed. "Maybe the next time I program this I won't work so hard to make sure she gets out."

CHAPTER 6

About ten minutes before John Craft tapped both Tim and Kelly on their backs, signaling them to exit VR and get on with their afternoon chores, he watched his genius brother tearing around the barn on his Toro lawn mower. After a minute or two on the sidelines, John Craft shook his head in frustration. He didn't understand genius, and after watching his brother slide around a particularly sharp curve he decided understanding it would probably take more energy than it was worth.

But something was bothering him, and he wanted to talk to someone about it. "Morty, get off that thing," John said as his brother came around again.

Surprised to see John, Morty Craft smiled, waved, but went around one more time before shutting off the engine and letting the lawn mower roll to a stop at his brother's feet. "Hi," he greeted. "Goes like mad, doesn't it?"

"You've got an IQ approaching two hundred and you're doing this?"

"Great, huh? I've got an IQ approaching two hundred, and I can *just* do this."

"I'm sure there's logic in there somewhere, but I don't have time to find it. Let's talk."

Morty slapped an affectionate arm on John's shoulder as they walked toward the house. "Okay, spill it, big brother."

"Are the kids inside?"

"I guess. They've been programming VR, and I guess they're trying out what they've come up with."

"They're farm kids, Mort. My kids. I count on them to work and do a good job. It's part of being a farm family. Otherwise

I have to hire people, and that takes money away from the family—too much money."

"And they're spending too much time . . ."

"They're minds aren't on their work. They're making mistakes. Minor ones now, but they could become major, and I don't have the time to watch after them."

"So you want me to talk to them?"

They were in the house now, standing in the living room. John Craft could see the two black suits; one stood like a hood ornament with hands and arms stretched to the side and behind as if tied there; the other was reclining.

"I want to know how to compete with what's in there."

Morty slapped his brother's back lovingly. "You can't. Believe me."

"What is in there?"

"What do you want to be in there?"

"It's like that, is it?"

"I'd be loving it if the government wasn't telling me I have to love it. Instead, I'm rebelling."

"But it can't go on like this."

Morty nodded understandingly. "Talk to them. Tell them how you feel."

"And how do I feel?"

"Well, let's see. You feel that life's a balancing act. That's it. A balancing act between where God puts us and what God puts in our hearts to encourage us to travel to our next destination."

"So God has put them on the farm, but he has also put in their hearts a desire to program silly little games."

"To create and explore. That's how they see it."

"God has made me a father and a farmer—that's all. Sometimes I don't understand what anyone can see in fantasy."

"Just talk to them."

John Craft nodded. This was going to be hard. There were times now when his kids seemed like strangers. They had done so many interesting things, such as meeting the president of the United States. Kelly had even become friends with the president's son. *She's only thirteen, and she knows people like that.* Yet God had made him their father, and as a father it was his responsibility to teach them right and wrong and God's perspective on that.

"Well, pray for me, Mort."

Morty nodded and watched as his brother went into the computer room and slapped each of his kids unceremoniously on the back.

◻

The afternoon milking ritual was about half over. They had finished milking the first ten cows and had just hooked up the second ten. "What do you think about what Dad said?" Kelly asked her brother, who leaned against one of the stalls.

"He was mad."

Kelly nodded. She had sensed that, too, that her father was angry, but when it came to running the farm—the family livelihood—their father could get very angry. Running the farm was serious, and their mistakes had serious consequences. They both knew this.

"He's right, you know," Kelly said. "We have to be more careful."

"He just wants us to spend more time working on the farm and less time learning about computers."

"He didn't say that."

"Sure, he did," Tim said flatly.

"No, he didn't. He said that he doesn't give us all that much to do, but what we are asked to do he expects us to do well."

"That's not what I heard."

"Well," said Kelly, "it's what I heard. Remember when he said that Jesus was a carpenter at fourteen."

"Like he was there."

"Well, I'm going to be more careful."

"And I'm going to get back into VR as soon as I can and make things happen."

The second ten cows were done so they hooked up the next ten. When they were done, Kelly asked, "How far have you gotten?"

"In VR? Not far. I've just been looking around in places the computer created." He hesitated, about to tell her that he had seen Sonya, but decided against it.

"I nearly got fried by the computer," said Kelly. "I programmed it one way, but the computer changed things."

"Computers don't—" Tim was about to say that computers don't change things, when he realized that the computer certainly had added things to his program, and adding them was just like changing them. "What changed?"

"I had Prince Charming—"

"You're kidding. You programmed a Prince Charming?"

"It wasn't really a Prince Charming, it was a White Knight—why am I explaining this to you? But I had him programmed to draw this big hammer; instead he drew his sword. The hammer came out later."

"You probably just programmed it wrong—changed your mind or something. When things are easy, they're easy to mess up."

"I guess," said Kelly, not satisfied but unable to come up with any other ideas.

The next set of cows was hooked up and the milk was flowing when Kelly said, "I'm going to the youth group meeting tonight."

"Let me know how it goes."

"Dad's serious. You ought to give it a rest tonight. Come to the meeting."

Tim laughed. "I'll do my chores. I can do what I want if I do my chores."

"Sure. Right."

"It is right," Tim said. "You've got your Prince Charming, and I've programmed a dream I've had too. I want to live it. And believe me, there are no cows in it—anywhere."

Kelly only nodded. But it wasn't agreement; it was just a nod that said their conversation was over. She liked VR as much as Tim did, but she also felt deeply about her responsibilities. Her father didn't overwork her—but he did count on her. She liked that.

She decided not to let him down.

Dinner at the Craft house ended about six-thirty as it always did. At six-thirty-five Tim began to drift toward the front door. "I'm going over to Uncle Morty's for a little while," he told his mother, who was working in the kitchen. His father had gone to finish some work he had in the shop.

"I thought you were going to the meeting."

"Not tonight. I've got something I want to do."

"You sure?"

"I'll be home early."

"Well, okay."

Tim didn't wait for her to change her mind. A second later the screen door was slamming.

"Are you going to the meeting?" her mother asked Kelly.

"We have to leave pretty soon," Kelly answered. "I'll get someone to drive me home."

During dinner, when the conversation had lagged, Kelly began to think about Prince Charming. Since she had read that novel about knights and princesses, she had dreamed of being swept off her feet by a Prince Charming. But now that the prince had actually saved her, her heart wasn't fluttering. Was it because he was a cartoon? Unreal?

Maybe.

After all, she gave Tim a hard time about Sonya—but that guy who betrayed her at the virtual CIA carnival when she and Tim were trying to get the president out of VR—he was cute. So she was capable of responding to a virtual Prince Charming—why wasn't she responding to this one?

She thought about that through most of the youth meeting. What was the use of being able to create a Prince Charming if you couldn't believe he *was* Prince Charming when he arrived?

A definite problem. Her thoughts about the prince came to an abrupt end when one of the kids laughingly suggested, "Maybe Kelly could ask the president's son to work at the booth."

They'd been locked in a brainstorm trying to come up with a way to promote the gospel while also promoting the farm way of life at their booth.

"Sure—Gar would love it," Kelly said sarcastically.

"Gar? You call him Gar?"

"Sure she does," came another voice. "He gave her a rose."

"A white rose."

"White? White means something. What does it mean?"

"It means it was the closest rose when he grabbed it," Kelly said flatly. But she could feel the blush on her cheeks. It *was* the closest rose, but he didn't have to reach for it, nor did he have to give it to her. But he had given it to her, and she loved that rose. She'd kept it, pressed it in her Bible.

"I saw your boyfriend's picture in the paper this morning."

"I saw it too. Maybe he'll come to Wisconsin."

That's when Pastor Cliff Switch came to her rescue so that by the end of the meeting Gar's name had only been mentioned another ten or fifteen times.

When she got home Tim hadn't returned yet. Kelly went up to her room. She was no longer thinking about Prince Charming. She was thinking about Gar. Taking the rose from her Bible, for a moment she took in its aroma, now growing faint. It wasn't quite dry yet, just flat, and she rolled it in her hand. One of the thorns stuck her, but she didn't care. After inhaling its sweetness again, she returned it to the Bible.

Did he like her? How could he when she was just a farm girl? But she had proved herself. She had saved his life—sort of.

But she'd probably never see him again anyway, and soon he'd be old enough to date and then he'd find someone else and she'd lose forever what she had never had.

In a way, Gar was her Prince Charming. The son of the president of the United States—maybe he would come and see her. Chicago wasn't all that far from Wisconsin—not for one of those small jets.

Gar—Prince Charming.

Sure.

"Mom," Kelly asked as she hit the bottom of the stairs. "Is today's morning paper around?"

"Why?" But then she understood. "Gar's picture. It's on the porch. Should be at the top of the stack."

She quickly found it, tore out the picture, and took it upstairs. It was about nine-thirty, and they had to get up at five. It had been a very full day—being nearly electrocuted at a tree could wear you out.

Where was Tim?

Oh, it didn't matter. He was wandering around his dream world somewhere, and Dad would be waking him up from it any minute now. She was going to sleep, and sometime tomorrow, as early as she could, she was going to meet her real Prince Charming. She closed her eyes with that wonderful thought swimming around in her head.

Tim returned. After their father chewed on him for being late, she heard his heavy footsteps coming up the stairs. She heard him rummaging around in his room for a second or two, then she heard his steps scampering down the hall to her room. The door swung open.

"You still awake?" he whispered.

"Like I could sleep with the elephant stampede out there."

He slipped in and sat on the edge of her bed. "I've been programming."

"I thought you'd already done that."

"I did, but then I lived a little of one of them—a football thing—"

"You don't play football—you're too skinny."

"I'm not skinny—I'm wiry. I'd make a good end. I can catch and run—you know I can run. It's something I always wanted to do. Every guy wants to be a football hero." He stopped. He was getting off his point. "But then I realized I could be so much more—a king of a country—I could be anything I wanted. No matter how far out."

"What are you doing then?"

Tim only smiled. "Maybe I'll show you later."

Kelly sighed. "I'm your sister."

"That's why I *might* show you later. Well, I'm tired—really tired. I'm going to keep programming tomorrow. It's going to be awesome."

"I need to sleep, and I have a dream I want to have—so good night, brother dear."

"If I wasn't so tired I'd sneak over to Uncle Morty's again tonight."

"I'm going to sleep."

"Maybe I could force myself to wake up early—"

"Give it a rest, Tim."

Tim left Kelly's room and went to his own. He climbed into bed but couldn't sleep. He was too excited. It wasn't so much that the world had opened up to him—the universe had. Virtual Reality could take him anywhere his imagination wanted to go. And he'd come up with a way to travel most of it and have an exciting time doing it.

From his desk he grabbed a tablet of paper and pencil and started taking notes. An hour later, he started designing with blocks and diagrams. An hour after that, his universe began to fill.

During the second set of cows, Tim fell asleep. He had been fighting to stay awake through the early part of the cow-milking ritual, but he succumbed as he leaned against the pipe stall. Kelly had gone into the milk house to check on the valve just one more time. She had checked on it earlier, but by the second ten cows she was sure that she had only dreamed that it was closed. When she returned from reassuring herself she found her brother, eyes closed, breathing heavily, with his arms draped over the top of the stall.

Heaving a great sigh, Kelly stepped up to him. Knowing that there was a pile of hay beneath him, she grabbed both of his hands and tossed them back over the stall. Without his hooks, he toppled to the floor. He woke up about halfway down.

Lying in a heap, he looked up with startled, though tired, eyes. "Huh?" he groaned.

"What happened?" she said in mock surprise. "Did something wake you? Like work, maybe?"

"I got to bed late."

"You didn't go over to Uncle Morty's again?"

"No. I just had a hard time putting my design down. I'm going to go back to programming it this afternoon."

"If you can keep your eyes open."

"When I get into VR I come alive."

"When Dad catches you sleeping in here you'll also come alive."

"You have a point. I tried to quit and go to sleep—about eleven, I think. But when I closed my eyes I thought of something else and I had to write it down. Then that led to something else."

"You're getting addicted to the computer."

"I am not. That's stupid. I just have ideas. I'm creative—maybe even an artist. Artists can't tell when they'll get an inspiration."

"Dad'll give you inspiration."

"Why would I do that?" came their father's voice from the milk house door. His large frame cut off most of the morning light. It was hard to see his expression, but from his tone it was probably stern.

"Uh," Tim began, "we were just talking about role models in life."

John Craft laughed softly. "Sure you were." But he let it drop. "How's it going?"

"Good," Kelly said. "We're about ready to start the third set.

I've checked the valve twice," she added, just to let him know she was trying.

"It looks okay," he reaffirmed as if he'd just gotten through checking it himself. "You get enough sleep last night?" he asked Tim.

"Slept like a baby," Tim said. He had. From about two until five.

"Good," their father said, but there was still just a hint of disbelief behind the word. "I'll be out in the field for the rest of the morning, so I'll see you guys at lunch."

Tim liked that news. He wouldn't be checking on them again, and they could lighten up a little. He might even be able to take a nap. No. A nap could wait. He wanted to get to the computer.

As it turned out, Kelly had some programming she wanted to do too. And some digitizing. So when the milking was done and the equipment cleanup finished, they headed over to their uncle's. They were a little surprised to see Elvira on the front porch.

Uncle Morty's single cow did have the run of the place, but she was discouraged from extending her domain to the areas where the humans lived. Oscar the beagle must have decided she belonged in more luxurious surroundings because when Tim and Kelly stepped onto the porch to see what was going on, Oscar stood before Elvira, his face laughing with contentment.

"Should we just leave her here?" Kelly wondered.

Tim shook his head and grabbed the cow by her halter. He then led her toward the porch door and down the stairs.

They found Uncle Morty in the repair shop. It was not a place Uncle Morty went very often, but he was working on a small motor. "I called the Toro lawn mower people. They told me how to increase the engine's compression. I should get a little more power out of it."

Tim and Kelly nodded.

"Elvira got onto the porch," Tim told him.

"She didn't sit on any of the wicker furniture, did she? I found her sitting on the little couch last time—left quite a dent."

"No," Kelly assured him, "just standing there."

"Well, put her out to pasture. You guys going to work in VR?"

"We both have some programming to do," Kelly told him.

"You two aren't getting too involved in VR, are you?"

"What's too involved?" Tim asked, a challenge in his voice.

"Where you're neglecting things you ought to be doing," Uncle Morty said firmly.

"You mean like sleep?" Kelly said for her brother's benefit.

"No," said Tim. "We're fine."

"Well, keep that in mind. God has given you a farm to help with as well as a talent for computers—right now the farm has got to come first."

"Right," assured Tim.

"We'll see you in a little while," Kelly said as they both turned and walked toward the house.

Tim got into his black VR suit, but before he zipped it up, he noticed Kelly standing by the tall, cylindrical digitizer. "What are you doing?" he asked.

"Digitizing something. Don't worry about it. You just go about doing what you're doing."

Tim only shrugged. He had too much to do to think about some weird thing his sister might be up to. He locked his zipper and waited as the visor came down.

Tim had found that the best way to program the Virtual Reality machine was from the inside. That way he could quickly test his ideas without having to get in and out of VR. When the visor was locked in place and the inside came alive, Tim simply said, "Do programming."

A programming console complete with display monitor, keyboard, and mouse appeared. He sat at it and began working.

A few minutes later Kelly did the same.

A half hour later Kelly got to her feet. She was finished and ready to try out what she had done.

Butterfly wings flapped in her stomach. She was nervous—probably more nervous than she had ever been as she prepared to try something new. In VR, the programmer can ask the computer to bring her into a specific place in the Virtual "story."

Kelly did that. So when her visor came alive again she was tied to the old dead tree at the top of the hill. The storm cloud above her was preparing to spit that immense bolt of lightning that would surely fry her. The White Knight stood beside her and was in the act of grabbing for his small dagger. In a single stroke, he sliced the ropes that bound her, pulling her away from the tree. They both dove down the side of the hill.

An instant later the cloud spit its humongous charge of electricity. As before, the tree burst into flames and splintered from tip to root. Smoldering pieces of wood fell around Princess Kelly and her knight.

"Are you all right, milady?" the White Knight, her brave Prince Charming, asked. He quickly jumped to his feet and extended a helping hand.

Her heart hung suspended in her chest until her hand took his and he lifted his visor. Looking down at her with those same, intense green eyes was Gar Harkin. "Please, allow me to help you up, milady," Gar said, firmly grasping her hand.

"With pleasure, my prince," said Kelly.

Now this was more like it.

CHAPTER 7

Are you all right, my daughter?" Kelly's bewhiskered virtual medieval father asked as he and Sir Edwin crowded around her.

"Fine, sure, just fine," Kelly said, eager to dismiss him. "Maybe you guys could take care of the Crimson Knight over there. Drive him a few more feet into the ground. Prince Charming and I have to talk."

"Prince Charming?" the White Knight said, those wonderfully green eyes confused. "I go by the White Knight."

"Sure, you do," Kelly said to him with a fetching smile.

"May I be so bold as to remove some of this armor, milady?"

She nodded. Great, it was all going just right. "Then we can take a walk. The rain has stopped, and look how quickly the clouds are disappearing. Oh, look, flowers, and more flowers." *That's one of the great things about VR—seasons can change quickly and very nicely.*

As she spoke, the world around them did just that. Whatever the season before, now it was spring—a colorful, sweet-smelling spring. She had programmed that. Walks with Prince Charmings require springtime.

Gar removed his helmet, and Sir Edwin helped him remove his breast, back, and leg armor. When they were finished, her Prince Charming was much smaller, but also much more as she remembered him.

"Thank you for saving me," she said, batting her eyes at Gar/Prince Charming.

"I should be thanking you," he said.

"Why?" she asked, puzzled.

"You have brightened my day more than any sun. Whatever danger I endured was a small price, indeed, for basking in your glory."

Now that was good. The conversation monitor she had defined for Gar was working quite well. Quite well indeed.

"You're too kind, my prince."

"I am not a prince, milady."

"You are to me," she said, her heart fluttering.

"Where should we walk?"

"There's a grove of blossoming cherry trees near here that leads to a lovely lake. I've always wanted to walk there with a knight who's saved my life."

Actually, there was such a place not far from the Craft farm. It wasn't a long lane, and it wasn't on their property, and sometimes, because the trees had been unpruned for several years, there were times when the blooms weren't quite so beautiful; but even for all that, it was truly a wonderful place in the spring. Kelly had walked through it to the lake a number of times wondering if, when she got older, she'd ever walk down it with the man of her dreams.

"Well, milady," Knight Gar said, "shall we enjoy your cherry blossom lane?"

Tim worked feverishly, and all the thought he had put into the design the night before quickly paid off. Within an hour of entering VR, he was ready to test his new universe.

Tim called himself "the Hunter."

He liked the name. It suited him and what he did.

Straddling his Galaxy Cycle, a Harley-like spaceship able to pierce the speed of light, he hunted the universe for those in trouble, for those in need of his special abilities. He had no fear. There was no need for fear. He could pulverize anything with his bare fists.

Streaking through endless space, his inexhaustible air pack on his back, two hoses feeding his transparent helmet, he heard a distress signal. A thin, hopeless voice calling to anyone who might be listening. "We're on Alpha Omega—eighth quadrant—help us, please. It might be coming back soon."

The voice repeated its hapless message several times, then the thread of sound died away in despair.

It was what he had been waiting for.

Having located the origin of the signal, the Hunter punched in the appropriate coordinates. Then the computer took over. It guided him past stars and remnants of stars, past moons, planets, comets, and clusters of deadly asteroids toward a single dead, parched-looking rock swirling in space. Tim intended to make the rock more jungle-like, maybe even beautiful, but first things first.

What could possibly be on that? the Hunter mused. The Hunter didn't know, but Tim the programmer did, and as he streaked through the thin, breathable atmosphere, heating up only enough to let him know it was there, his heart began to pound anxiously. Everything was working perfectly, so he knew someone was waiting for him.

The rock was just that—a world of rock. Rock everywhere. All browns, reds, yellows—usual rock colors. Tall piles of rocks, short piles, slabs jutting out from flat, table rocks. Tim never had much imagination with rocks. That's why he thought a jungle would be an improvement. But that would come later.

Finding a long, flat spot near the origin of the signal, the Hunter landed, the two tires of his cycle touching ground together. The Hunter, his eyes peeled for someone in danger, dismounted the Galaxy Cycle and prepared himself for whatever lay ahead.

Scanning the horizon in all directions, he thought he saw something out of the ordinary—something non-rock—visible between two piles of rocks in the distance. It glistened with brilliant red and white and looked metallic.

Remounting his Galaxy Cycle, the Hunter eased it toward the rocks. Pulling alongside he dismounted again. Now closer, he saw that it was a rocket's tail section. Stepping quickly between the rocks, the Hunter was presented with a gruesome sight. The rocket had apparently tried to land but then skidded along the ground, stopping only when it slammed against this wall of rocks. Around it were patches and streaks of what looked like blood, some smeared savagely on the rocket's hull, some staining and streaking the ground as it led away from the crash site. The signs of blood told of violence, as if bodies had been dragged away, kicking and maybe screaming, to the base of a huge slab of rock at the edge of this arena-like formation.

The survivors signaling for help must be in the spaceship, the Hunter thought. Though the ship was crumpled on its belly, the door appeared undamaged. Crossing to it, the Hunter slapped an open hand against it. When he heard nothing, he slapped again.

A woman's voice, maybe a girl's, called from inside, "Who's there?" The voice sounded thin and as hopeless as the one he had heard from space.

"I am the Hunter," Tim announced.

"I'm sorry, but we don't want any today."

The Hunter groaned. "You're not supposed to say that, Sonya."

The door opened wide, and Sonya stood there in a silvery jumpsuit. She frowned. "I'm just having fun. The damsel in distress stuff just isn't me."

"But you said you'd—"

"Okay—okay. Say your line again." She slammed the door.

"I am the Hunter."

"The Hunter? Oh, you've come. I'd hoped you'd come. I'm the only one left. All the others have died or been killed. Now that you're here my prayers have been answered. . . . Did you write this?"

"Just say your lines! I have my Galaxy Cycle outside, and we can get off of this rock together."

"I don't think so," said the girl. The door slid open a crack and a thin, frightened hand emerged. It pointed to somewhere in back of him.

The Hunter turned. "What's there?" he asked.

"Just wait a minute and you'll see."

The slab of rock at the end of the bloody paths began to rise, and as it rose a deep, guttural growl rose with it—a growl that had to be from some heinous beast.

"He's coming," Sonya whispered, all the terror of the ages surging through her words.

The computer did too good a job with the growl. It was deep as Tim had programmed it, but it seemed deeper than deep—so deep that it resonated through his very bones, rumbled through his brain like the very essence of fear. Although the Hunter was fearless, Tim Craft nearly croaked!

But Tim had no time to be frightened. He quickly gathered his courage together and fashioned himself into the Hunter again. Standing tall, he watched the slab rise slowly, revealing an empty, fathomless darkness behind it. But the darkness remained empty for only a moment. The monster appeared. Standing upright, its head was a massive combination of pit bull and lion, maybe nine feet tall and muscular. Its arms were long, like an ape's, but its hands had many wiggling fingers, fingers meant for grabbing, arms meant for carrying things to its teeth, and teeth meant for tearing bodies to shreds. The total monster.

The monster growled. With no rock to muffle it, the growl resonated like thunder. It tore through Tim's head and turned the courage there to mush.

He was about to turn and run when he remembered who and what he was—and what he was capable of doing.

"You can't fight him," came the cry from within the spaceship. "Run. Save yourself. Don't worry about me." Then the Hunter heard a small giggle. "This should be good."

The monster stepped into the light. It looked even more menacing with all its muscles and the flame of rage in its eyes highlighted.

The Hunter who knew no fear swallowed hard. Clenching his iron fists, he moved in.

The monster swung one of its long arms. The Hunter lithely ducked. The monster grabbed at him, but the Hunter dodged and weaved. The monster swung again. This one connected. The Hunter was knocked back and nearly fell. His shoulder hurting where he'd been hit, he moved back in. The monster grabbed at him, and this time a couple of those wiggling fingers caught him. The Hunter knocked the hand away but not before the fingers wrenched his arm. That hurt too. The monster wasn't supposed to hurt him like that. Kelly had said the computer was doing some things on its own. Maybe it was doing that here too. It was time to end this before the monster scored any more points.

Fists clenched, the Hunter leaped forward and slammed the monster right on the snout. Nothing could survive the Hunter's punch to the snout, so the monster reeled, spun as if in some kind of grotesque ballet, and dropped like a sack of potatoes.

The door to the spaceship flung open, and the girl ran out. Throwing grateful arms around the Hunter's neck, she looked up into his eyes. "You were wonderful. Just wonderful. I've never seen anyone as brave as—" She stopped. "Don't you think I'm laying it on just a little thick? I mean, you did a good job and all, but you did program it so you'd win."

"Sonya," Tim said with great frustration, "you said you'd do it right."

"But I didn't think you'd have me saying things like this. I'm not a talker, anyway. I do things." And with that she wrapped her arms around his neck and pulled him to her.

Tim was caught by surprise, and although he liked the idea of her affection, sometimes when she carried out these little plans of hers he found himself getting embarrassed. Not only was he embarrassed this time, he was also still a little mad at her for messing up his dream. So, when those arms closed around his neck, he pulled them away. "Now, stop that," he protested.

"You don't like it?"

"Not all the time."

Showing some frustration of her own, she turned and looked at the fallen monster. "This is silly, anyway."

"Silly?"

"Sure. You create a monster to fight, but you know you can beat it."

"What kind of fun would it be if the monster won?"

"Not great, I guess. But it still seems dumb."

"Dumb? Well maybe you don't want to be a part of the other stuff. Maybe you'd like to be an eighty-year-old woman again. Maybe I ought to give you one leg or two noses—just think how cute you'd be with two noses."

"Fortunately I don't get colds."

Tim softened slightly, though he was still angry. "I'm the programmer here. Not you. You said you wanted to help, so I let you. Then you ruin it."

Sonya's hand slipped into Tim's.

He halfheartedly tried to pull it away, but her grip remained firm. "I didn't ruin it. Just lightened it up a little. You can get very serious, you know. Come on, admit it, it was more fun with me here, wasn't it?"

"Yeah, I guess," he said reluctantly. "But this is just the first part of the adventure. You ought to see what I've got planned. And if you want to be a part of it, you have to be good."

"See, you are too serious—me? Good?"

"Sonya, this is important to me," he said, pleading.

"Okay, I'm sorry."

He studied her for a moment and saw her big almond eyes looking up at him. She looked sorry. But part of her look still seemed to say, "I'm not a bit sorry, and I'm going to have fun anytime I want and particularly when you don't expect—or want it." To his surprise, that part of her made her look even cuter.

"So you promise to play along?" he stated, just to make doubly sure.

"Whatever," she said, her smile big.

"Do this again, and you're out."

"Okay, already. You want me to sign in blood somewhere?" Not waiting for him to answer, she asked, "Where to now?"

Tim hesitated. "We'll leave that a surprise."

"Oh, Timmy, you know I don't like surprises."

"You love surprises. Everything you do to me is a surprise. I'm the one who doesn't like surprises."

Sonya poked a playful finger into his chest. "You're catching on," she said with a coy, mischievous smile.

"Okay, you go to wherever you go when I'm not around—"

"I wait."

"Well, go wait. I've got more to program. It is a big universe that God's given me, and this was only a small part of it."

"Do I have to be another damsel in distress? I just don't fit that part."

"You'll see later."

"Well, if I'm going to wait I don't want to wait here. I'll see you later."

Sonya poked him again in the chest, winked, and faded into nothing.

Tim took the opportunity of being alone again to look around at what he had created. His arm still hurt, and he reached over and rubbed it as he looked at the monster's crumpled heap. He had programmed the monster to lose, there was no doubting that, but he, the Hunter, had fought him. He had taken a couple of blows—the ache in his upper arm was proof of that. Sonya was wrong. His dream wasn't silly—or dumb. He had actually lived it. He'd actually traveled the universe looking for someone to help—how great was that! And the next installment would be even better!

With that in mind, he said in a clear voice, "Do programming." Instantly the rock world faded, and a display monitor, keyboard, and mouse appeared. With hardly a moment's hesitation, he started programming again.

Although the rock world faded as far as Tim was concerned, it still existed for Hammond Helbert. He stepped out from behind the crumpled spaceship and strolled over to the monster's massive body. His plan was definitely coming together in his mind. A plan that would get the revenge he wanted without those kids even knowing he was there. That way he could escape and never even be sought by the authorities. There were still details to work out, but as he looked down at the monster the Tim-boy had created, the main points were taking shape. With a kind of laugh, he planted a foot on the monster's chest and smiled. *How'd you like to win next time, ol' boy?*

CHAPTER 8

Kelly didn't want to leave Gar, but she knew she had to. She had to do her chores, and she was getting a little bored anyway. The lake was beautiful and the cherry blossoms were picture perfect—the computer tended to make things that way—and Gar was everything she'd hoped he'd be.

But he wasn't real.

And he behaved like a Prince Charming instead of like a fun fourteen-year-old guy. Yet that didn't make pushing her palm button any easier.

As she climbed out of her black suit, she noticed that Tim was still seated at his programming workstation—he looked foolish sitting there with no chair. But she probably looked the same way when she was programming.

What would she do next? Tim was the one with all the imagination; she had her share, but she often wondered if she hadn't been shortchanged in that department. Being rescued by her Prince Charming was about all she wanted.

No. There had to be more. Maybe while she was working on her chores before lunch—straightening up Dad's toolshed this morning—she'd think about it. Or maybe she'd just think about the wonderful green eyes. She had spent extra time describing to the computer what those eyes looked like, and the computer had done a wonderful job. They even looked better than Gar's. or at least how she remembered them to be.

"You're home," her mother greeted as Kelly walked into the kitchen.

"I was just going to give Dad's toolshed a once over."

"He's in there now. The tractor had distributor problems this morning—or something like that."

As Kelly was about to step out the back screen door, her mother said, "I almost forgot. Pastor Cliff called. He wanted to have another youth group meeting tonight. He said something about a project you guys are working on. Since it's Friday, I invited them all over here. I thought we could barbecue hot dogs or something, and you and the kids could play volleyball by the pond. Is that okay?"

"Sure," Kelly said. "It'll be fun." She said the word *fun* as if she wasn't sure.

She found her father bent over his workbench. The toolshed had only a single light over the workbench itself that lit the rest of the room dimly. There was a high window, but it was dirty and let in little light. "Hi," she greeted, stepping up to him.

"Hi, yourself."

"I thought I'd clean up in here now."

"You can work over there for a while. I won't be long."

"Mom says it's a distributor."

"It's dirty. I'm cleaning it."

Kelly nodded and started straightening things up on the opposite side of the room.

"How's your virtual world?" John Craft asked while he worked.

"Okay," she answered. "It's sort of like living in a book."

"What book were you living in this morning?"

"A Knights of the Round Table kind of thing." She answered in a tone that didn't invite more questions. Her father must never know that Gar was now in her program. That would be too embarrassing.

"Sounds like fun."

"I'm really trying to make sure I put my chores first," she said, not sure why she suddenly felt like defending herself.

Hearing her tone, her father stopped his work and turned. "I'm sure you are. I guess I've been a little worried. I know you're only thirteen and probably not thinking about things like this, but I guess I'm a little afraid I'm losing you guys. I love you and Tim with all my heart, and I always thought I'd have you nearby all my life."

"What about college?"

"Oh, I knew you'd go off to college, but then I figured you'd come back. Either work this farm or get one nearby—maybe the old Higgins place, that deserted farm up the road. But now that you're so involved in computers and with all those powerful people—well. I'll miss you two, that's all."

Kelly knew exactly what her father was saying. She was thirteen, and she had thought about not coming back to the farm after college. Right at this moment she hoped it would be Gar Harkin who swept her away from the farm, but it would probably be someone or something else. She'd miss her father too.

"We're not going anywhere," she said, knowing that at least a part of her was lying.

After giving her a smile, her father went back to the distributor and she to straightening up. A couple of minutes later her father announced that he was done and said he was going to check on a few things before joining her in the house for lunch.

Five minutes later he returned to the toolshed. Even in the dim light she could easily see that he was not happy. Not one bit.

"Is your brother at Uncle Morty's?" he asked.

"In VR," she replied. "What's wrong?"

"Did you help him clean the milking equipment this morning?"

"We each do half."

"Does his half still have the glass milk collector in it?"

Kelly nodded sheepishly. They each always did the same half, so there was never a fight or anything missed.

"I guess yesterday's talk with him didn't sink in," her father stated.

He marched out the toolshed door angrily. A moment later Kelly heard the car engine grind to a start. Dad only took the car to Uncle Morty's when he was in a hurry. *He must be really angry,* she thought.

About the time his father had found the glass milk collector still coated with the morning's milk—a place bacteria loved to call home, Tim decided it was time to stop programming and get home. He didn't want to upset his father any more than he had already. This morning had been close. He'd gottten through the milking only because it was second nature to him. If he'd had to think about what he was doing, he would have been in real trouble.

But he felt okay now. His little adventure on Rock World, as he had started to call it, had been fun, and programming new things was exciting and got his adrenalin pumping.

After hanging up his black suit, he stepped outside to find Uncle Morty installing his newly souped up engine on his Toro lawn mower. "How's it going, Uncle Morty?"

"Okay—it's going good. Ought to run like mad. The race is tomorrow, you know. Are you coming down to see it?"

"Sure—of course."

"How's your programming coming?" Uncle Morty asked, taking a break and sitting down on the lawn mower's seat.

"Good. It's fun."

"Can I take a look sometime?"

"Sure," Tim said, but giving his permission felt uncomfortable. "You can't criticize, though. It's sort of my dreams—things I've always wanted to do."

"Can I give advice?"

"Okay—sure."

Uncle Morty gave him a good-natured smile. "The best advice I can give you is don't forget the Lord in there. He's where all the good dreams come from. And he's certainly the one who makes them all come true."

"Right," Tim said. After a moment of self-conscious hesitation, he headed off across the fields toward his house.

He heard a car honking when he'd gone about fifty yards. The road wasn't far away from the field, and he was surprised to see his dad standing beside the car and motioning for him to join him.

When Tim was about ten yards away, he realized that his father didn't look happy—quite the opposite.

The lecture was quick. John Craft never minced words. He always said exactly what was on his mind, and when the word stream ended Tim knew exactly where he stood. "We're playing no games here, Tim. That dirty piece of equipment could have shut us down. The milk would have been contaminated. Best case, we would have lost two day's production, because it would have contaminated what we did yesterday that hasn't been picked up yet. Worst case, the health inspectors might have shut us down completely. You've got one more chance. I'll be checking after each milking for the next week. One mistake and the only reality, virtual or otherwise, you'll be experiencing will be the inside of your room. Understood?"

How could Tim not understand?

"Yes. I'm really sorry. I thought I got it all."

"You didn't. Now let's go home for lunch. You'll be working on the farm—our farm—all afternoon, so you won't be going to your uncle's again today. Is that understood?"

"What am I doing?"

"I don't know yet. But believe me, I'll find something. And whatever it is, it won't be easy."

Tim had seen war movies where the guys in basic training were required to scrub their barracks floor with toothbrushes. He had always thought that was a little excessive. But, as the afternoon wore on, he began to believe those army guys had it easy.

His job that afternoon was to clean—"I mean clean," his father had said—the milk barn, the milk house, and all the milking equipment. "I want to be able to eat off that floor without a plate. Understood?"

His dad had started putting "understood" at the end of his instructions lately. Tim didn't like it. But he liked working like this even less. After he'd been slaving for about an hour, his dad returned from the fields and showed him a buildup of dirt in the crack between the cement floor and the walls and how to dig it out. An hour later there were more filthy revelations.

His dad had a knack for punishment. It was always memorable, always fit the crime, and always hard. This one was no exception. In fact, it was so severe that Tim was even happy when Kelly came to visit.

"Maybe you'll get a good night's sleep tonight," she said, standing in the middle of the milk barn and looking around. "You're doing a good job. I'll recommend to Dad that you do this at least once a week."

"Maybe we ought to trade off."

Kelly shook her head. "No. You've got the talent. Exploit it."

"Yeah, right."

"Did Mom tell you that Pastor Cliff and the youth group are coming over here tonight."

"Really? Why?"

"Mom invited them. We're going to have a barbecue and play volleyball."

"I wonder how many volleyballs will end up in the pond."

"None if you don't play. But that's not why I brought it up."

Tim now looked interested. "Why did you bring it up?"

"You know that I have this little weak spot in my heart for Gar. Right?"

"Weak spot! You turn to mush."

"Well, the kids seem to like kidding me about it."

"Something worth encouraging."

"Well, that's just it. I don't want you to encourage it. I don't want you to even mention it. You have to say you'll do that for me."

"But why would I do that for you?"

"Because you're my brother, and I saved you from swamp snakes not long ago."

"The swamp didn't exist. How could you save me from something that didn't exist?"

"The pain of that snakebite existed, didn't it? So would one of those alligators taking a bite out of you. I've saved you a bunch of times. Now I want you to pay me back. And believe me, if you don't, the next time you sit on that Harley, the seat's going to develop teeth."

"Ooh! Nice. So if I don't mention Gar tonight, then we're even for all the good things you've ever done for me—ever?"

Kelly thought for a moment. "I think that's a fair trade, yes."

"You programmed Gar into VR, didn't you?" Tim said, eyes studying her.

"I nev—" she stopped. Lying was not easy for Kelly. "How did—"

"You digitized the picture in the paper." He laughed a knowing, slightly malicious laugh. "Were you walking hand in hand with him? Whispering sweet nothings into each other's ears?"

"I should have let those snakes devour you. Especially that big one. I wonder how the VR suit would simulate you being digested. No. We only talked—and he sort of saved me from being hit by lightning. You're such a baby sometimes."

Tim softened. "I'll keep my mouth shut. I'm not going to be there for all the meeting anyway."

"You're not? You're going back to VR?"

"Dad's got me working all afternoon. But not tonight."

Kelly's eyes narrowed. "Tim, are you sure you're not addicted to that computer? You really are starting to worry me a little. I know how hard it is for me to leave, but I'm trying not to let it get to me. It *is* hard to stay away."

"What if I am addicted? So what? It's not like drugs or anything."

"It might be if you let it take over."

Tim only shrugged. "Anyway, I won't be mentioning Gar. Unless someone asks," he said, trying to sound good-natured.

Kelly didn't smile back. She was becoming concerned about her brother, but she was even more concerned that he might only be kidding about keeping his mouth shut about Gar.

They finished the evening milking without a hitch. Their dad even complimented them on how quickly they finished. He also told Tim he appreciated his work on the milk barn. "It looks great—really good." Although Tim was still a little put out that he'd had to do it in the first place, he did appreciate his father's approval.

Since dinner was going to be delayed until Pastor Cliff and the kids got there, Tim was able to grab a quick nap. For about an hour he slept like a rock.

He actually woke refreshed.

The coals in the barbecue were glowing by the time Tim came downstairs and joined his parents and Uncle Morty on the side patio. They sat on the wooden patio furniture, each with a lemonade. June Craft's lemonade was legendary in Chippewa Falls. Not only were the coals glowing, but the hot dogs and hamburgers were stacked and covered on the shelf beside the barbecue. Bug candles were lighted everywhere and seemed to be doing a reasonable job.

His mother poured him a tall glass of lemonade as Tim walked up. She told him, "Everybody's due in a few minutes. Kelly's back there on the swing. She seemed a little pensive. Do you know why?"

"I'll go see."

"Your dad said you did a great job on the barn today," Uncle

Morty said before Tim had a chance to leave. "You worked hard."

"I hope I'm an inspiration for your lawn mower race tomorrow."

Morty nodded and toasted him with his glass. "Here's to inspiration."

"I don't know who I wonder about more," Tim's dad said. "Him and VR or you and your lawn mower."

Tim just toasted his uncle back and walked behind the house. Kelly wasn't in the bench swing. She was draped over the old tire swing that hung at the edge of the pond. As little kids they had loved that swing. They used to sit inside the tube, drape their arms over the top, and their mom or dad would swing them out over the water. Sometimes they even dove from it when it was far out over the pond. When they got bigger, though, the bench swing took over.

"What are you doing here?" Tim asked, walking up behind her. "That rope's a little old."

Kelly grunted.

"What's the matter?"

"You'd only tease me."

"Gar?"

"See."

"I'm not teasing you."

"Sure you are. The tone of your voice."

"What tone?"

"It's there. A kidding tone."

"You're nuts. What about Gar?"

"Do you think he likes me?"

The question caught him a little off guard. He wasn't sure how honest he should be. "What's the difference?" he finally said. "The guy's half a country away."

"That doesn't matter. I'd like it if he were sitting in the White House mooning over me like I'm mooning over him."

"He's in Washington, D.C., living with the president of the United States. I doubt if he's mooning about anything—stars entertain at the White House; he can probably see any movie he wants—just orders it. I doubt if he even *wants* to leave the White House. But then if he does he can probably take a jet anywhere he wants. Nothing to do? Off to Disney World. Mooning? Not likely."

"You sure do have a way of making a girl feel better," Kelly said, trying to emphasize the sarcasm.

"Maybe letting *him* save you from lightning wasn't such a good idea."

She didn't have a chance to answer because a couple of the youth group kids called from the side of the house. "I got dibs on the tire after Kelly," one yelled.

"You'd break the rope," the other piped.

Kelly spun the tire around to face them and waved halfheartedly.

A couple of guys arrived right behind them. They came around the corner of the house already holding plastic cups of lemonade. "Where's the volleyball?" they asked.

"You're just anxious to get beat."

"Tim, where's the volleyball?"

The rest of the group arrived within the next few minutes and a little while later, just after the volleyball game got started, Pastor Cliff got there. The fun really started then. Pastor Cliff loved a good time, and he was determined that *everyone* was going to have one when he was around. The game went crazy. The only things flying faster than the ball were the jokes, and the only thing louder than the kids' screams was the laughter.

John Craft stepped around the corner of the house to ask when he ought to put on the hamburgers. To encourage his kids' involvement in sports and to make a place for groups to meet, he had built a grassy volleyball court and an asphalt basketball half-court in the back of his home near the duck pond. His plan had worked. Whenever there was a youth group party in the works, his place was the first suggested. But what he saw now troubled him a little. Neither Kelly nor Tim looked like they were enjoying themselves. While the other kids were bouncing around like Ping-Pong balls, his two were standing in the corner of the volleyball court waiting for the ball to come their way. Patience is not a virtue in volleyball.

Kelly's patience, however, was rewarded—but she didn't react quickly enough. The ball bounced off her shoulder and into the pond. It skipped once, then floated toward the middle. A couple of ducks charged it and started their own game.

"Sorry," Kelly said feebly.

They grabbed another ball that lay nearby and resumed their game.

"Pastor Cliff," John Craft called. "I'm putting on the burgers."

"Could you put 'em on in ten minutes—if that's okay?"

"Ten minutes."

John Craft returned to his chair and took a sip of lemonade. "You ought to see our kids," he said to June. "They're standing around like statues. Not playing at all." He turned to Uncle Morty. "This is your fault. You and that machine of yours."

"Think so?" Uncle Morty said.

"They were fine until they started messing around with it."

"It if weren't VR, it would be something else."

"You're pretty casual about this, Morty," John said.

June placed a warm hand on her husband's arm.

But John went on, "The Lord gave me a farm and a family. It's my responsibility to take care of one in order to feed and raise up the other. That machine of yours is making it tougher than it ought to be."

"It's a novelty," Uncle Morty said. "They'll get tired of it soon. I know I have."

"You'd be in there with them if it hadn't become work," June said with a good-natured laugh.

"True enough. But they're creative kids. Like I was—am. I'd get involved with something new—attack it like a shark—then move on. They'll do the same."

John Craft wasn't convinced. He took a long drink of lemonade, batted away a gnat, and studied his brother for a minute. "And what kind of witness are you for the kids?" he finally said.

"John," his wife injected, "that's not nice."

"What's that mean?" Uncle Morty asked his brother.

"God wants us to work. He gives us responsibilities and gifts, and we are to use one to fulfill the other. He has given you a brain like none I've ever seen, and you're frittering it away on lawn mower races."

"John," his wife injected again, "you know that Morty has done a great deal for his country. He deserves a little rest."

"It's not about rest."

"John," Morty began, but then stopped. "I'm tired. I've been working on that report and preparing for the race all day. I think I'm going to get some of that rest June says I deserve."

"Are you sure?" June asked. But before he could answer she

heard the phone ringing inside. "Oh," she said, still hoping to convince Morty to stay, "don't leave until I get back."

June answered the phone in the kitchen. "Hello," she greeted.

"Is this Mrs. June Craft?"

"Speaking."

"Mrs. Craft, this is Bill Harkin."

There are times when even the most familiar names don't connect. It happened to June Craft this time. "Yes, Mr. Harkin, can I help you?"

"Do you know who I am?"

"No." But suddenly the name clicked. "Bill Harkin, the president?"

"I have got a favor to ask."

Five minutes later June Craft stepped out of the kitchen, her expression a battle between Christian reserve and excited awe.

"You okay?" John asked. "Who was on the phone?"

June held up her hand to silently ask her husband to wait, then walked to the corner of the house where she could see the volleyball game. Her husband had been right; Kelly was playing, but she was playing listlessly. Well, June had some news that should change that.

"Kelly," she called.

Kelly's eyes came up.

"Come here a sec. I've got something to tell you."

Kelly looked a little puzzled but left the game and ran up the shallow incline to her mom.

One of the kids called out, "Maybe Gar Harkin's on the phone."

Before they finished laughing, Kelly asked, "What is it, Mom?"

Before her mother could answer, Kelly's dad came around the corner of the house. "There's a caravan of limousines coming up the road."

Kelly's eyes narrowed, then widened in disbelieving hope. She eyed her mother, then her father, then, overwhelmed by an anxious impatience, she ran around to the front of the house.

When the other kids saw her take off, they all followed. They rounded the corner just in time to see the first of three black limousines pull into the drive. It came up to the barn across from the house and stopped. Two men in dark blue suits emerged and surrounded the second limo which came up to the house and stopped while the third stopped just behind it. From the third, two more men in dark blue suits emerged, and they took up positions around the car.

The rear door of the car was opened from the inside, and a fifth man in a blue suit stepped out. He stood beside the door, and, as Kelly's heart jumped into her throat, Gar Harkin stepped out.

CHAPTER 9

Gar's face lit up when he saw Kelly. "Kelly," he said, "I was just in the neighborhood."

Behind her Kelly heard oohs and ahs from the kids.

"It's really him," one of the girls gasped.

Kelly's mom was right behind her and whispered, "The president called—Gar's spending the weekend."

Kelly wasn't sure whether her heart was still beating, but she managed a big, welcoming smile. "Hi," she greeted weakly, not sure what else to say. "Wanna play some volleyball?"

"Great," Gar called back as they walked toward one another.

Kelly thought he looked as good as ever as she met him on the front lawn. "I didn't think I'd ever see you again," she said when the others couldn't hear.

Gar got a sweetly shy glint in his eyes. "I kept looking for a way to get here—and finally found one."

As her father met with the Secret Service people, Kelly led Gar over to the youth group. After introducing Pastor Cliff, she went down the names one by one. The kids were in awe as Gar greeted them in return.

"Where's Tim?" Gar asked after the final introduction.

That was the first they realized that Tim was missing. "He said he had to go to the rest room," Pastor Cliff said. "Maybe he's sick or something."

Kelly just shook her head impatiently. "He's busy." Then turning her attention back to her visitor, she said, "If you're staying the weekend, you'll see him later."

From then on Kelly had a hard time keeping her eyes off Gar. Not that she tried. And, for all her scrutiny, he faired pretty well.

At the barbecue Gar ate and joked with the other kids. He played volleyball well but was no star—he fit in well with the rest of his team.

Once, losing sight of the out-of-bounds line, he chased a volley over it and almost chased it into the pond when he stopped, his toes balancing on the edge. Only the quick action of one of the guys who grabbed his belt and pulled him back prevented him from falling in. Everyone, including Gar, had a good laugh about that. Then he came up with the winning suggestion for their booth at the meeting.

"I'm no farmer," Gar said, after listening to the discussion and ideas for a while. "Maybe you could show all the things farms depend on the Lord for and how the Lord takes care of them. He sure has taken care of me," he added, casting shy eyes toward Kelly—nobody missed that. She could have both killed and kissed him at the same moment.

When Pastor Cliff endorsed the suggestion, the others passed it unanimously.

◎

"I don't like it that Tim took off like that," John Craft told Morty as they sat on the side patio with the three off-duty Secret Service agents. The other two were with Gar in the front room.

"Not so fast. The more I think about it, I might be making a mistake not using your son."

"Using him how?"

"Well, he suggested it once, and I turned him down. Tim probably knows more about VR than I do right now. Maybe I could use his experiences in my reports. Maybe I could avoid ever going in there again."

"You mean pretend as if you did the work? You see nothing wrong with that?"

"It's all in how you word things," Uncle Morty said. "I won't take the credit—or really say I did it. There's no use in Tim's efforts going to waste. Tim, maybe Kelly, too, will discover imaginative and constructive ways to use VR."

"He still should have been here for the meeting."

"I'll talk to him tomorrow."

"What's in VR that captures a fourteen-year-old boy's imagination like that?"

"I don't want to bother you," one of the Secret Service men

asked as he ate his second barbecued hamburger, "but is there any more lemonade? It's good stuff."

"Sure. In the refrigerator inside. Help yourself." John turned his attention back to his brother. "What in heaven's name is Tim doing in there?"

Tim had finished his programming and was now ready to make his first run. He was excited. This was going to be fun—strange, but fun.

The Hunter rode his Galaxy Cycle into deep space. It was a place where stars were born and died and no one ever knew. Where worlds collided and no one cared but God, who kept it to himself.

This was God's universe.

Now Tim was rocketing into it, seeing what only God had seen before.

Actually a genuine feeling of awe was sweeping over him. No one had ever before seen what he was seeing—not even he. The computer had created it from the smallest of instructions. It had done a good job too.

Before and around him was an endless cathedral of lights—small, large, pinpoints, and swirling galaxies, clouds of stars and gases—all against the blackest black. He couldn't see enough of it and was actually lost in exploring when the distress call came.

It took him a while to realize that it actually was a distress call coming over his radio, for not only was it breaking through a busy, preoccupied mind, but it didn't *sound* much like a distress call—not till later, anyway.

"Does it work?" it began.

"The light's on."

"What light?"

"That little one there."

"So we might be transmitting now."

"Maybe."

Tim listened intently and found himself grinning. It was clear why these two, whoever they were, were in distress. They certainly weren't prepared, technologically speaking, to be in deep space.

"But what should we say?" one voice went on.

"I've got an idea."

"An idea, Graham? That's trouble."

"My ideas got us here, Wheaters. Didn't they?"

Each emphasized the other's name as if piling on the ridicule.

"Well, okay, Graham, what's your idea?" Wheaters said, sounding conciliatory.

A pause as if Graham were taking a deep breath. Then, "HELP!"

"Is that all you could come up with?"

"What's wrong with it? It says it all."

"Just (screaming) HELP! (regular voice) It doesn't say anything. The person who hears it might think we just need help with our laundry. He wouldn't know that we're being attacked by tyrants and may die any minute. Saying that needs more than (screaming) HELP!"

"Like what? What more does it need?" Graham's voice hardened.

"Well, like (pause to catch breath, then screaming) HELP! HELP! WE'RE BEING ATTACKED BY TYRANTS AND MAY DIE ANY MINUTE," Wheaters told him. "Like that. See. Says it all."

"Should we put in that we're about to be buried in exploding cherries and drowned in a tidal wave of chocolate?"

"No. The tyrant part is good enough."

"Do you think anyone heard us?"

"Out here?" Wheaters groaned. "Not likely."

"So the (screaming) HELP! (regular voice) might have been enough?"

"But it wouldn't have said it all."

"But if no one's listening . . ." Graham's voice trailed away as if even more confused.

It went on like this for a while. Long enough for Tim, the Hunter, to determine precisely where the signal was coming from. Punching the throttle and easing the Galaxy Cycle around, he headed for a point in the universe where he'd never been.

This was going to be good.

After what seemed like a long time but was probably only five minutes, he began to notice a spot against the black backdrop far in front of him. After a few minutes, it began to take shape. And what a shape it was. He had expected round. All planets were round, or at least round enough, but even though this one may have had a round foundation, its features were exaggerated and irregular. Huge mountains stuck up on all sides like party hats, some of them in groups to form ranges; there were flat plateaus and formations that looked like tall sundae dishes. Cutting between all that were deep, sometimes broad, valleys. The computer had been given some general information and came up with this.

Strange place, Tim thought. *The computer's got a sense of humor.*

But he was sure he hadn't seen anything yet.

As he broke into the warmth of the atmosphere, shapes took on identities, and the colors became curiously vivid. The mountains were definitely mountains, but they didn't look like any he had ever seen before. Instead of craggy peaks and faces of chiseled rock, they were piles of what looked like scoops of stuff—stuff of different colors: rich pink, dark brown, a white now and then, sometimes a white marbled with golden brown.

Wow, look what it did.

Some of the mountains were sleeker; instead of piles of scoops, they looked more like traditional ski slopes. At their summits the snow didn't lay evenly as Tim would have expected, but it was piled in huge globs as if topped with a spoon. All over them were occasional outcroppings of brown.

"It looks just like it ought to look—wow!" the Hunter exclaimed.

Rivers cut through the valleys. Sometimes waterfalls leaped from high ledges to crash into pools below. The rivers and waterfalls were brown or gold or deep ruby red.

The verbal sparring on the radio ended, but the Hunter had already determined a general area to look for the men in trouble. They seemed to be located somewhere in a deep river valley cut by one of the brown rivers, between two mountain ranges. He rode carefully down into the valley, expecting to hear the thunder of his cycle echoing back and forth. But the sound was swallowed up by the cliffs on either side, giving it an unearthly quality.

Below, the brown river gurgled; on either side of it the land was a consistent toasty color. The cliffs on the right were piles of scoops and on the left were sleek. Now and then a canyon branched off from the main one, the river of brown cascading from it to meet the main river.

It's perfect, Tim mused.

He was almost down to the river, but he hadn't seen or heard anything when something round, red, and about the size of a basketball cannoned past his nose. Whatever it was slammed into the hill on the other side of the valley. But he didn't see it fall, nor did he see it splat and half bury itself in the ground.

He didn't see it because another red thing smashed into the side of his Galaxy Cycle. Another *splat!* Whatever it was struck him on the knee, split, and the goo inside ran down his leg.

It smelled sweet—like cherry juice. Just like it was supposed to. The computer had put all this together with so little information. It was unfolding just as he'd hoped, yet it was all still a surprise.

Another surprise. He'd been knocked off course, and the goo had fouled his engine. It began to cough and sputter. He was falling!

Another red thing struck him in the rear of the cycle, causing it and him to spin. Now, not only was he falling, but he was spinning out of control. He heard cheering. Whoever had attacked him was cheering the successful attack.

The ground came up pretty fast. The Hunter hoped he would fall into the river, even if it was brown. But he wasn't going to. Preparing himself for impact, he cringed, closed his eyes, and said a prayer. Seconds later he spun into the ground.

Though he had been going at a pretty good clip, his Galaxy Cycle didn't shatter. It cut into the ground like a drill, boring a broad hole deeper than he and the cycle were tall. When it finally stopped, he lay in an impression against the wall, the cycle at his feet.

Suddenly he didn't care about the hole. The ground had taste, or at least smelled as if it did. Rich, like vanilla. But he'd made a mistake. He had created something that probably tasted good that he couldn't taste—VR couldn't simulate tasting.

The gooey red stuff on his pant leg also had an aroma. "Cherries," Tim said softly.

He grabbed a handful of "ground" and sniffed it again. "Cake. The computer made it cake."

He was about to test a thick vein of dark brown when a head popped through the hole wall. The head had cherry red hair and wide, startled eyes. His mustache and beard were covered in crumbs. "You've got to be here to save us," the head said.

Before Tim could answer, another head popped out about a quarter of the way around the hole from the first head. This one had nut brown hair, the same startled eyes, and a crumb-encrusted mustache. "Certainly he's here to save us. Why else would he be here? You're responding to my perfectly worded message, aren't you?"

"It couldn't be that perfectly worded or he wouldn't have ended up here."

"Here? Where's here?" Tim asked.

Both heads looked mystified. "In a hole," they replied.

"No. Where am I?" Tim asked again.

Again the heads looked at each other mystified. "You're here."

"What planet am I on?"

"Planet?" the beard asked.

"We're on a planet? What's a planet?"

"Never mind. Who are you guys?"

The beard said, "I'm Graham—that's Wheaters."

"Graham's our king," Wheaters said, his voice sounding just a little bitter.

"Well, Graham and Wheaters, is this cake?"

"Cake? What's that?"

"It doesn't matter."

"Then why ask it?" Wheaters asked, quite befuddled.

"He's still groggy," Graham suggested. "He did get cherried!"

There was an explosion above and the ground shook. Great chunks of cake broke loose and fell on them. Tim and the cycle sank a little deeper.

"Cherry bombs," Graham said, eyes up respectfully.

"Fizzy-water injected in the cherries. They explode on impact. The ultimate weapon."

Another bomb detonated, and the ground shook again. Tim and the cycle sank further.

"We have to get out of here," Tim demanded. "We can talk later."

"Good thinking," Graham said.

"If it came from someone other than you, it is."

Graham ignored Wheaters. "You'll have to follow me. Kings always lead."

"That may change," Wheaters muttered.

Graham didn't hear him or chose not to react. "Dive in behind me and start digging," he said.

His head popped back into the cake, leaving a small hole behind him. Tim quickly crawled over his cycle and dove into the hole. Now he knew how a mole felt. Graham left a small tunnel in his wake, so it was reasonably easy to follow him. But Tim had to enlarge it, so he was constantly digging to make the way bigger. He wished VR allowed him to stuff some of the cake into his mouth. It smelled wonderful.

Tim heard a voice. "Keep moving. Graham is pulling ahead of you. You don't want to lose him. The ground fills in the hole quickly."

Tim glanced over his shoulder and found Wheaters behind him keeping within inches of Tim's scrambling feet.

"How far?" Tim asked.

"Not far. We're under the great Sundae Range now."

Tim had to laugh. *Sundae Range. That's rich—the computer has a sense of humor.*

No more than five minutes later Tim saw Graham's feet. They'd stopped working. "Go up alongside of him," Wheaters said to him.

Tim did and Wheaters was right behind him. Now three heads, Tim's in the middle, poked out from the cake. Tim looked down and immediately felt a little dizzy. They weren't far from the summit of a very tall cliff.

"Don't say it," Graham insisted.

"You cherry-head. You've got nothing in there but juice."

"I'm king. You shouldn't talk that way to me."

"You've been digging your whole life, and you end up here?"

"What's happening?" Tim asked, hoping to quiet them.

Wheaters replied, "We should be down there."

On the valley floor below was a small village. A huddle of buildings was randomly located near the edge of the brown river, their rich orange roofs bright against the light brown earth. The people scurrying around looked quite small.

"Maybe it's good we're here," Graham said.

"How is that possible?" Wheaters protested.

"We can show him the threat."

"What threat?" Tim asked.

Graham pushed a hand out away from the cliff and pointed off to the right.

A tall, broad dam constructed of something that looked like more cake spanned the little valley. The dam, though, was only part of the picture. Towering above it on the right was a huge white mountain, its summit cloaked in rivers of brown and what looked like clouds of whipped cream. Cutting across this mountain, beginning high on his right side and continuing to a point just above the dam, was what looked like an immense sugar wafer. *The computer has a sweet tooth,* Tim mused.

"What's behind the dam?" Tim asked.

"About a billion tons of chocolate," Wheaters told him. "It's a reservoir. We tap into it in the summer when things go dry. If the dam goes, it'll wipe us out."

"Wipe *everything* out," Graham corrected.

"Of course, it'll wipe everything out, but we're the important things."

"It's important to emphasize—"

"Sure, sure, sure," Wheaters said impatiently.

"What's the dam made of?" Tim asked.

"Fruitcake," said Graham. "It's really dense, and nobody eats it—ever."

"Then what's the threat?"

"Cherry bombs," Wheaters said gravely. "A few placed just on top, and it'll crack like an egg."

"The mountain dwellers have decided to wipe us out," explained Graham.

"Why?"

"They met Graham," Wheaters said darkly.

"They didn't like me," Graham admitted. "I've no idea why."

Tim only nodded. "So everything on this planet is made of cake and chocolate," Tim said, looking for confirmation. He'd told the computer to build a planet of goodies. It had.

"And ice cream and whipped cream and butterscotch and caramel and strawberry toppings and nuts," Graham said thoughtfully.

"And cherries—and fizzy-water," added Wheaters.

"Blast that fizzy-water," Graham exclaimed.

"Our world was a lot safer without it," confirmed Wheaters.

"Where does fizzy-water come from?" Tim asked.

"There's a pool of it on that mountain over there—the one overlooking the chocolate—Mount Calorie," Wheaters answered.

"We need to get down to the village. There are maps and things there," Graham said.

"Yours aren't right," Wheaters injected.

"Sure they're right."

"Guys, we need to get to the village. We can make plans there," Tim said authoritatively.

After digging back down through the cake, the three of them emerged from the cliff only a few feet above the valley floor.

"I would have hit it on the nose," Wheaters told Graham.

"You keep this up, and I'll hit you on the nose."

They began walking toward the village. Graham's and Wheater's unending jabs at one another continued until they'd nearly reached it.

Their banter ended, however, when the villagers began to emerge from the houses and run to greet them. Before Tim knew it, he was surrounded by at least a hundred men, women, and children. They began to cheer him. But there was more than cheers; there was adoration and bowing and tears. To them, Tim was obviously someone very special.

"Our savior, savior, savior!" they began chanting.

"Jesus is savior," Tim corrected, feeling immensely self-righteous. "I'm just a programmer." But it made no difference. In fact, just after he said it, the crowd around him began to part—an aisle opening. At the end of it stood Sonya.

She wore a gown of purest white with what looked like gumdrops sewn all over it like sequins. Standing regally, she carried a white pillow before her. Resting on it was a shiny, ornately carved, chocolate crown bejeweled with hundreds of Jelly-Bellys.

Graham gasped in disbelief. "That's my crown."

"Not anymore," Wheaters said with a note of triumph. "You've been a boob long enough.

Carrying the crown carefully, Sonya walked up the middle of the aisle. When she reached Tim, she stopped and waited. Her eyes riveted proudly on Tim. "Now this is cool," she muttered with an appreciative nod.

Knowing that he had no choice, even though his heart was breaking, Graham took the crown with both hands and placed it gently on Tim's head. The instant it was in place Sonya took her place beside Tim, and the crowd went ballistic. "I guess they want you instead of me," said Graham.

"Can you blame 'em?" Wheaters injected.

Sonya leaned toward Tim. "I wasn't sure if I was supposed to carry that crown or eat it. Really neat place."

"I thought you'd like it," Tim said, glad she was impressed.

"Skiing's gotta be a kick here. Fall down and eat your way home."

"Your majesty," Wheaters began, "shall we go to your throne room?"

"Just a sec," Tim said. He turned back to Sonya. "Been here long?"

"Just waiting for you."

"What's happening with the Mountain People?"

"You have to do something. If they blow up that fruitcake—everything goes."

Tim studied the dam for a moment, then the mountain beside it. "I can hardly wait to do battle on a pile of ice cream."

"It won't be as much fun as you think—you'll get very cold feet."

At that instant someone knocked on his back from outside the VR suit. His fun was over. Since he had left the youth group thing without saying anything, he knew there would probably be a lecture about that, then there'd be bed and milking again. Then he'd come back. The Mountain People would be made to pay for bothering *his* people.

Tim pressed his palm button and vanished.

Hammond Helbert watched it all. He stood on a distant mountain, his feet planted firmly in cold vanilla ice cream, and his mind worked overtime.

His plan was complete. Every bit of it—all the details, all the traps, all the pain, all the final devastation. When Tim came back in the morning, it would be all ready for him—then the Kelly-girl, then that ridiculous uncle of theirs.

All of them.

In twenty-four hours this little matter of revenge will be settled—and the machine will be mine.

CHAPTER 10

Crash!

The Jenga tower crumbled. The little oblong blocks slid in all directions on the kitchen table as Gar pulled a block from the bottom of the stack. Jenga was a simple game. Oblong blocks, each the same size, were stacked three to a level. The levels crisscrossed. The idea was to take one block at a time from the lower levels and place it carefully on the top. The player who removed the block that made the tower fall lost. This was the sixth game Gar and Kelly had played, and they were tied three and three. Gar had never played the game before, but he was definitely holding his own.

He hardly took a breath before he started building the tower again preparing for another game.

"You think you're actually going to win?" Kelly chided him.

"Not if I keep blowing it like that."

When the tower was half built, Kelly's mom stepped in. "I don't mean to break things up, but, Kelly, you have to get up early. Your dad's already gone to get Tim."

"Only one more game," Kelly pleaded. "We're tied."

"That's the best time to stop—you're both winners."

"But, Mom."

"Time to put it away," her mother insisted. Kelly sighed, but started boxing the Jenga game.

"Where is Tim?" Gar asked. They'd been busy since the end of the youth meeting and the kids had disappeared. Tim's name hadn't come up until now.

"He's in VR."

"Virtual Reality? Really?"

"The machine's at Uncle Morty's house."

"I like your uncle. He did a lot for my dad and me."

Morty Craft had been held prisoner by Hammond Helbert with the president and Gar in VR. At the time Gar and his father hadn't been getting along, but Uncle Morty had helped them start communicating again.

"What's Tim doing in there?" Gar continued.

"He won't say, but he's a good programmer—or at least he says he is."

"He's programming?"

"I am too."

"Really? I was never able to do very much. And what I did do that Hammond Helbert guy messed up."

"Would you want to, after your last trip?"

"It wasn't VR's fault what happened."

"In that case, maybe we could take a little trip through there. I can show you what—"

"Guys," came her mother's voice again. She sat on the porch working on a quilt. "I've set up the guest room for Gar."

A Secret Service agent was sitting in the living room, his eyes never wavering from Gar, no matter where he was. Another one was in the barn loft keeping his eye on the house and surrounding area. Three others were already sleeping at a motel in town and would return to relieve these two at midnight.

But none of that concerned Gar.

"Can I help you in the morning?" he asked Kelly, who placed the Jenga box in the pantry.

"Tomorrow's Saturday, so we get up at six for milking. You sure you want to do that?"

"Sure. I've never milked a cow before."

"Don't think you're handicapped now. Your life might actually be better off."

"No. Dad always says that farmers and the farming work ethic are the backbone of the country."

"It might be the downfall of farm kids though."

"You don't believe that," her mother said as she stepped in from the porch.

"The cows are in the meadow too. That means we have to round 'em up in the morning and get them into the milk barn. That's always fun."

The Secret Service agent was on his feet now and heading to

the stairs where Kelly and Gar stood. "I'll just take one of these kitchen chairs and set up in the hallway," he said.

"Good," Kelly's mom said. "A chaperon."

Kelly blushed.

▣

Few words were spoken between Tim and his father as they walked back to the house. Tim knew his dad was upset. But then, he was always upset lately. While lying in bed the night before, Tim had developed a theory why: His father was jealous.

Instead of the farm being the most important thing in Tim's life now, VR was. His world was a lot bigger now. And his father resented that.

"Tim," finally came the voice Tim had expected. "I'm getting worried."

"What about?"

"Your behavior."

"What about it?" Tim asked sullenly.

"You sneaked off from the meeting."

"I had to go to the rest room, and on the way back I had an idea I wanted to try out. I got over there, tried it out, it worked, and then I got a little involved."

"You're allowing that computer to take over. It's not so much the time you're spending—which is considerable—but it's the way you're letting it—well—just take over."

"It's not taking over."

"Sure, it is. The youth group came over tonight to discuss an important outreach. They're trying to do something new. And instead of concentrating on that—just for a few hours—your mind was taken over by a computer game."

"It's more than a game."

"See. I've told you about a problem, and rather than answering me, you're defending the machine. I didn't even want you to go in there today. That's why you were given the job of cleaning the barn. But I guess I didn't make that clear. So I'll clarify it. Tomorrow is Saturday. I don't want you in VR tomorrow—Saturday—any time it is Saturday."

"But, Dad. Things are finally starting to come together."

"No, Tim, they're starting to come apart. And I have the obligation to make sure things don't. I want you to take a rest, just for tomorrow. You'll do your normal work and live your normal life as if that machine didn't exist. Understood?"

Tim didn't even nod. He just sighed and turned to his father. "I guess I'll see you at the house."

His father could easily match him stride for stride, but when Tim decided to walk ahead, his father let him go.

But when Tim arrived home he found a man in the loft who called to him as he approached the porch. "Who are you?"

"Me? I live here. Who are you?"

"You Tim?"

"Yes, but who are you?"

"Go on in."

"Who's that?" he asked his mother when he stepped onto the porch.

"Secret Service."

"Why?"

"Gar's upstairs."

"You're kidding "

"Did the man in the loft sound like he was kidding?"

"Well—at least he fits right in. No one kids around here anymore. I'll see you in the morning."

Maybe because of the scowl on his face, Tim was actually frisked by the guy in the second floor hallway. But when the humiliation was done, he went into his room and went to bed.

For Kelly, Saturday was magic.

She and Gar were inseparable. Although the Secret Service had their doubts when Gar announced that he wanted to help Kelly round up the cows in the morning, they didn't interfere. And it really didn't go that badly. Then he helped Kelly with the milking. He helped gather up the equipment, helped hook up her half of the cows, and helped her clean up afterward. Since she had a guest, her mom relieved her from some of her chores, and she and Gar and some of the other church kids went down to the lake and played around.

For Tim, Saturday was the pits.

Struggling with the idea of defying his father kept him awake for a couple of hours Friday night, so when he awoke, he was again tired. He found no joy in Gar's presence. In fact, it bothered him. Here he was being kept away from the thing he liked, while Kelly got what she wanted—really wanted.

To cap it all off, he nearly got trampled herding the cows into the barn. It was one of those freak incidents that he had to blame the Lord for—who else would he blame? Something reflected the early morning sun and blinded him for a moment. Whatever it was was in the center of the old windmill blades on the deserted Higgins farm down the road. It blinded Tim just long enough for a couple of cows to change direction and trot across his toes.

Thinking that he had broken toes kept him awake during milking—that and the fact that his sister and Gar wouldn't stop talking. And the stuff they talked about—it wasn't interesting.

Jenga strategy—why are some of the blocks loose and others aren't? Should you take middle blocks or the end blocks and leave the middle ones? What if it falls before you touch it but after the other person's turn is done?

Come on, guys, who cares? Tim wanted to say—but didn't.

What if cow udders get stopped up? Would they explode? Or would it explode if you didn't milk the cow a couple of days running?

Come on, guys, it won't explode—ever—no matter what, Tim also wanted to say—but didn't.

Why does it smell like this?

It would smell a lot better if you guys stopped talking. He didn't say it.

But the babbling never stopped, and all the time he was trying to figure out what he could do to make sure the Mountain People in VR wouldn't hurt his Valley People. And what would it be like to swim through chocolate?

Finally he wondered what had reflected the light so brightly at the old Higgins farm that it had nearly blinded him. *Any metal on that old windmill would have rusted brown by now,* he thought.

He didn't go to the lake with the others. He didn't have a guest, so he ended up working a little harder than was usual on Saturday. Not only did he mow the lawn, but he helped his mother weed their large vegetable garden. The tomatoes were coming in in bushels, or what seemed like bushels, so he spent time picking them.

As it was, he forgot all about Uncle Morty's lawn mower

race. He didn't even think about it until Uncle Morty came by the farm for support. He had lost.

"I came in second," Uncle Morty said, his expression downcast.

John Craft listened from the barn while his brother told Tim what happened.

"But you souped up the motor," Tim said.

"I was outclassed. Actually I came in third, but I was gaining on her and would have beaten her if the course had been a few feet longer."

"A girl racing lawn mowers. And beat you?"

"Hard to believe, isn't it?"

"But you're a genius."

"I'm not so sure anymore."

"So a woman beat you," John Craft injected, coming out of the barn.

"She did," Morty replied, his shoulders slumping even further.

"If you'd won—what would have changed for you?" John Craft asked.

"Changed?"

"Sure. Would they have showered you with athletic endorsements? Or given you a trip to Europe or something?"

"I would have had the pleasure of winning."

"With that and a dollar you can get a cup of coffee."

"You're just not a sportsman," Uncle Morty said to his brother.

"Looks like you aren't either."

"Touché," said Morty. Then he turned to Tim. "You coming over later?"

Tim eyed his father, hoping there was still the possibility that his father might relent.

"No," said John Craft. "Not today. He's taking a rest from VR."

"A rest," Uncle Morty repeated. "Well, if you want to have a Coke and console me in my loss—"

"He can do that tomorrow—maybe," John Craft said firmly.

Tim didn't reply, but returned to his gardening.

The afternoon passed for Tim as if he were in jail and Disney World was outside his cell window. Close but untouchable.

After the evening milking, things got a little more exciting. A reporter from the *Chippewa News* came by to interview Gar. The reason for his coming, of course, was Kelly. Gar played that down because he knew what would happen if it got out that he had traveled more than a thousand miles to visit a girl. Kelly wouldn't have minded his saying it. She thought the limelight might have been fun.

But he resisted. Tim and Kelly were both friends, and he was in the neighborhood.

Several in the youth group showed up again for volleyball, then Kelly and Gar played some games and took a couple of walks.

For Tim the only thing that mattered was that Saturday was evaporating; the day was going where all old days go—it was becoming history. And when it did, his cell door unlocked.

At nine he began to yawn, and by nine-thirty he had excused himself. Setting his alarm for midnight, he crawled into bed and tried to sleep.

At midnight the alarm sounded. Having been awake since eleven-thirty, Tim quickly flipped the alarm off and told himself several times he was nuts—sleep was far more important than wandering around an intergalactic ice cream cone. But that sort of talk lasted only a few minutes. He crawled out of bed, slipped into his jeans, sweatshirt, and tennies, and opened his bedroom door.

The Secret Service man's head came up from a magazine he was reading. He said nothing, but his expression held a huge question mark.

"Restless," said Tim. "Going for a walk."

"Here? With all these cows around? Good luck."

Hammond Helbert had worked all night Friday preparing for Tim and the others. When Tim didn't show up Saturday he got a little concerned, but then he spied him working in the garden and figured that his dad had intervened. The kid would definitely be back, probably soon.

So he took advantage of the extra time to tighten the traps and make things a little more foolproof. He also knew that once his trap was sprung he'd be working nonstop until his whole plan had unfolded. So he also took the opportunity to rest. He felt like a fighter waiting for the bell.

The bell rang just a little after midnight. Hammond had rigged VR to signal him when Tim entered, so when the siren sounded just under his pillow, he was dressed and in his VR suit within ten minutes.

His time had come.

CHAPTER 11

Tim's eyes burned from lack of sleep and his muscles still hadn't awakened, but none of that mattered to him. He was in control again.

The visor dropped before those burning eyes, and VR came alive for him.

But he didn't reenter Goody Land, the land of ice cream sundaes, as he'd come to call it.

He entered back at the beginning where the Harley motorcycles were. Although they were exciting when he first rode them, they didn't matter much to him anymore. There were more interesting things to experience.

He took a couple of steps forward and noticed a piece of paper lying on one of the bikes. From where he stood he could see something written on it.

What was *this* all about? Was VR doing its own thing again? *Maybe the older it gets the more it learns? It's probably like me that way. Now it's learned enough to design a place like Goody Land and then do something like this to make my life miserable.*

But when he read the note he wasn't miserable anymore. It shot a bolt of excitement through him that awakened every muscle in his body.

It read:

This is Matthew Helbert.

You have learned to program my Virtual Reality machine, and I congratulate you. I have always worked alone, so I have never had the opportunity to be appreci-

ated by anyone I've worked with. Now I want to be appreciated by you. You are to be given a reward.

I have placed the greatest of my discoveries at the end of a virtual path. To find it, you must make it to the end, overcoming all that I place before you.

When you do, you will have wealth and be honored by the world as no one before you. I dislike such notoriety, so I've kept this for you.

Why you? Because, in a very real sense, you are lucky. There are a number of random number generators at work in VR. Every time you enter, they spin and produce a series of numbers. The numbers came up right this time. They have opened all the doors, and all you have to do is go through them. If you leave VR, the doors will close. Trust me, you will never have this opportunity again.

I'm thanking you for your commitment to my dream and asking that until you find it, you think of nothing else. You'll not regret it.

You will be told what to do along the way.

Now, hold this note tightly and say, "Make it happen."

All the best to you.

Then came what looked like Matthew Helbert's signature.

Tim read it again, then once more. Was it true? If it was, his life was about to change—more than change, be transformed.

Suddenly roaming around the universe saving beautiful maidens or strange people on ice cream planets seemed pretty silly. Matthew Helbert was a genius like Uncle Morty, but unlike Uncle Morty, he was an inventor—one of his creations helped battle leukemia, another was Virtual Reality itself. If what waited for Tim was the greatest of his inventions, then it had to be something extraordinary. And Tim's reward would also be extraordinary.

Wealth, fame, and all that went with them. He'd be on talk shows—maybe do a Disney World commercial. "Tim Craft, where are you going now?" "I'm going to Disney World." He'd get his own Jet Ski—Jet Ski nothing, his own *jet*.

And all this at fourteen.

Not bad for a farm kid. Not bad at all.

Tim stood tall and studied the note once more.

"Okay, Matthew, here goes."

He held the note tightly and said, "Make it happen."

The world around him faded, and for a moment or two he was completely in the dark. But then the world came to life again, and he was in Rock World once more. But this time he wasn't the Hunter. He was in his own street clothes, and the Galaxy Cycle was nowhere to be found.

He stood just outside the arena of rocks, the rocket's tail section visible.

He looked around for instructions. The note said he would be told what to do. Was he supposed to do what he'd done the last time?

Why not?

He walked over to the circle of rocks and stood by the tail section. There was no sound except a whine of wind. He hadn't noticed the wind the last time. Now it hissed across the rocks and added to a sense of desolation.

Was Sonya in the rocket?

He wanted to find out—it was suddenly very important. He stepped up to the rocket door and slammed a flat hand on it.

The door opened wide enough for a hand to reach out and give him a note. Then the hand disappeared behind the closed door. It looked like Sonya's hand.

The note read: "Lock the monster out of his lair and yourself inside it, and you'll be on your way."

Tim turned and looked at the slab of rock behind which lived his monster. He had to lure the monster out and sneak in and bring the door back down. It would take some intricate timing, but it probably wouldn't be too tough.

He knew he had written the program to lift the slab of rock and release the monster when Sonya said, "He's coming." So all he had to do was get her to say the words.

He slammed on the door again. "You in there, Sonya?"

"Whose arm do you think that was? You want me to come out?"

"Right. Come out and say, 'He's coming.'"

"The monster?"

"Come out and say it," he repeated.

"But the monster comes out then."

Tim looked again toward the slab of rock—the monster's door. "Just for a second. Let's talk face to face."

"With a face like yours?"

"Just come out here."

The rocket door slid open, and Sonya stepped out. She looked uneasy when she saw that Tim wasn't in his Hunter clothes. "What's going on?"

"I've got something I need to do, and you're going to help. I'm going to hide beside the monster's door. You say, 'He's coming,' and when he comes out I'll slip in and close the door."

"That means the monster'll be locked on the outside. And I'll be on the outside with him. I hate when that happens."

"But it's important."

Sonya laughed.

"But it is. Anyway, you're a computer character; you've got to do as I say."

"Where's that written?"

"In the documentation."

"Documentation or no documentation. I don't stand outside with monsters."

"Just say it, then run into the rocket."

"I'll starve in there before he leaves."

"You're a computer character, for crying out loud. You can't starve. Your stomach doesn't even growl. Now get a grip and do it."

Sonya looked at the slab of rock. "I really don't want to do it."

"You're a cartoon. He could rip your arms off, and it wouldn't matter. I'd just program you a set of new ones."

"But I'm programmed not to want my arms ripped off."

"Say, 'He's coming,' and say it as soon as I'm over there."

Tim ran quickly over to the side of the monster's slab door, hid behind a protruding rock, and prepared himself.

Sonya moved close to the rocket door and took a deep breath. Then, "He's coming."

The slab began to grind, rock against sandy rock, rising slowly.

Sonya didn't wait for the slab to lift but disappeared into the rocket and slammed the door behind her.

Tim watched her and made sure she was safe, then held his

breath, afraid to make a sound. The slab continued to grind up. Then the slab stopped. It was all the way open.

But no monster.

Tim continued to wait. Where was it? It should have come out when the slab was still moving. But it didn't.

Tim waited another minute. Finally he started breathing again. He found himself relaxing a little, leaning against the rock as if trying to make himself comfortable.

Two minutes passed.

How long should he wait?

This was strange.

Tim stood. Maybe he should peek around the corner and see what was going on.

He took another couple of breaths and decided to look. He eased up to the corner and pushed his face around it.

The monster looked back at him! That massive mix of pit bull and lion, those black eyes, those teeth meant for tearing. Although it was nine feet tall, it was stooping down, its face the same height as Tim's. They were nose to nose.

It growled—that deep, guttural growl that sent a shiver up Tim's spine. But the shiver was the least of his worries. What was he going to do? The monster's hands came up, and all those little fingers were now inches from Tim's neck. And the monster, sure that all it had to do was grab this little morsel and start tearing him apart, smiled.

Tim nearly smiled back. But he didn't have time. A hand with a thousand fingers on it came up and grabbed him by the shoulder. Nearly crushing his bone, the pain shooting into Tim's neck and chest, the monster lifted him up, then grabbed the other shoulder and brought Tim's face up to its own again. It smiled—then slammed him against a rock. The black suit simulated the impact well; it hurt—really hurt.

Holding Tim against the rock with one hand, the monster drew back its other hand and prepared to slam its fist right through Tim's face.

"Hey, bozo!"

The monster's attention turned, its expression a question.

Sonya stood in the rocket's open doorway.

"What do ya say, bozo?"

The monster roared. Keeping Tim pinned against rock, it twisted around.

"Get back in the rocket," Tim cried.

The monster roared like a lion and pushed its face back into Tim's. Fiery eyes burned into Tim's as it prepared that fist again.

"Hey," Sonya called. "I'm over here."

The monster turned completely around. This time it let Tim go to devote its attention to Sonya. Now free, Tim slid down the rock and lay on the ground in a heap at the monster's feet. A second later, the monster launched itself toward Sonya.

"Get inside!" Tim cried to Sonya, his shoulders still aching.

But she'd already spun and dived into the rocket. The door closed behind her, and Tim heaved a sigh of relief. She was safe inside.

Back, arms, and neck bruised, Tim prepared to stumble into the monster's lair and somehow close the door. But he didn't make it. The monster reached the rocket. It was as tall as the rocket, and it studied the machine for only a second.

Deciding on a course of action, it made all those fingers into the weirdest-looking fist and slammed it into the side of the rocket.

Tim couldn't believe it.

The monster drove a fist right through the metal. What would that fist look like to Sonya inside? All those wormy fingers reaching out blindly for her.

Sonya's reaction was what Tim expected. She screamed, the sound of it muffled by the rocket's metal skin.

"She's only a cartoon," Tim said to himself. "I can reprogram her no matter what happens to her."

But when the monster slammed its other fist through the metal, and then started to push the rocket back and forth to the terrible music of Sonya's screams, Tim couldn't just leave her—he had to do something.

Taking Sonya's tack, he cried, "Stop, bozo!"

The monster roared but didn't turn. Instead it did what even Tim didn't think it had the strength to do. With its arms outstretched and still buried in the rocket, the monster began to lift it. At first the rocket just shuddered under the strain, but then it rose a few inches off the ground. Then a foot, then several feet.

"And what are you going to do with that, bozo?" Tim shouted.

From inside, Sonya's frantic screams never stopped. What

must she be doing in there? Tim could almost see her trying to move as far away from those fists as she could, frantically searching for a way out—and finding none. Matthew had programmed her with a passion to survive—like any character, computer or otherwise—and now she screamed as the monster, taking one plodding step at a time, carried her off.

Helpless, Tim took a moment to evaluate his options as he rubbed feeling back into his shoulder. He didn't have any options. He could only follow at a safe distance until something occurred to him. He only hoped it wouldn't occur too late for Sonya.

Okay, where was that monster taking her?

One thing for sure, it was in earnest. It now lifted the dented rocket over its head and was moving laboriously through the largest opening in the rocks away from the crash site.

But where was it going? It had to be going somewhere.

Could Tim attack? With what? There weren't even any rocks to throw. Although this was a rock world, Tim hadn't programmed any smaller, throwable rocks. And even if he could have thrown a stone or two, the monster would have only set the rocket down, torn Tim apart, picked the rocket back up again, and continued on his way.

Thinking that he might be able to see something from higher up, Tim forgot his pains and climbed to the top of the tallest boulder. His heart caught in his throat. Not far off, maybe a five-minute walk for the monster, was a cliff. The monster was heading right for it. He was going to drop the rocket, with Sonya inside, over the cliff. With the lower ground beyond the cliff so distant, the cliff looked like a tall one.

Now Tim really had to act!

He scrambled down the rock and ran after the monster, staying a safe distance behind. Something just had to happen, something to give him an idea, or better yet, an opportunity.

The monster kept walking—almost like a robot—one step at a time, the cliff growing closer with each.

Lord, please. Or maybe you don't care about a computer character . . . this is crazy. She's a computer character.

A moment later he saw something move at the rocket's tail. Was part of the rocket coming loose? No. It was something protruding, then pulling back, then protruding again. Sonya? It was her head. Was there enough room for the rest of her? Her shoulders wouldn't fit. Yes, there they were. She saw Tim and waved awkwardly but went right back to work. She continued to shimmy herself out of the obviously cramped opening. She made little progress.

She would need more time—but didn't have it. The monster had reached the edge of the cliff!

Abruptly Sonya broke free! Her legs lifted out of the hole, and now she took a moment to assess the drop—about fifteen feet to the ground.

The monster pulled the rocket back, preparing to throw it down with force.

But before it could let the rocket fly, Sonya dropped to the ground. Hurt, she tried to scramble away, but her legs wouldn't work—she couldn't move.

Tim knew exactly what to do now.

As the monster turned its head to see what had dropped at its feet, Tim ran at it full speed. When he was within a few feet, he leaped up, feetfirst, and planted them on the monster's back. Tim bounced back and landed on the ground not far from Sonya. The monster, however, had been driven over the cliff. With a roar of terror, it toppled over the edge, the rocket acting like an anchor.

Tim and Sonya heard the rocket strike the cliff face on the way down, then hit the rocks below with a frightening explosion—so great that flames and smoke billowed above the plateau where Tim and Sonya sat.

"Monster fall down, go boom," Tim said.

"You okay?" Sonya asked.

"That's my line."

"I'm okay—my ankle hurts. It's always been weak—Matthew didn't like perfectly built people. It hurts."

Tim had pains of his own but decided not to list them. "Do you feel up to going with me?"

"I need to rest a while. You go on ahead. I'll catch up with you later."

"You sure?"

"I'll be fine."

"Good. I still have to get somewhere. A lot depends on it." Patting her hand, then waving farewell, he headed quickly to the monster's lair. He stepped inside and found a button on the wall near the door. After he pressed it, the slab of stone began to fall.

A moment later he was encased in a lightless black. He had fulfilled the requirements of the note. Now what?

Argh! Monster lairs smell horrible. Being a farm boy, Tim had smelled some pretty bad things, but nothing like this. He definitely wanted a short stay. Fortunately, after a few minutes, his eyes got used to the darkness, and things began to appear—walls, rocks, the depth of a cave.

Well, caves are for exploring, he thought. *Maybe the smell is better down there somewhere.*

Using his hands to feel his way, Tim started walking, cautiously at first, then after a short while his eyes became even more accustomed to the dark and he could see a little better. He began to walk with greater confidence.

Of course, when his confidence had returned completely, the floor of the cave unceremoniously dropped out from under him and he slid down a slick, steep incline. Instantly, whatever light there had been went out, and he was again cocooned in black. Also, the cave had been cooler than Rock World's surface; now it was getting downright cold, and the further he slid the colder it got. Finally reaching the bottom, he slid along a slick floor for a moment or two before coming to a stop.

The natural question arose: "Where am I?" He asked it several times as he got to his feet and felt around a little bit. The air was freezing, but the walls that surrounded him were even colder.

But they were not particularly hard. They had a slimy texture to them.

After exploring the walls for a few minutes, he found a passageway. He walked carefully, his hands reaching out in both directions to touch the walls on either side. After only a short walk, he came to a dead end, his nose hitting the end of the tunnel. But the wall his nose was buried in gave way. He pushed against it, and his hand sank up to his elbow—that arm was very cold now.

Maybe he could dig through it like the cake ground in Goody Land. Maybe he was actually back in Goody Land.

"Only one way to find out," he said to himself.

That was to try to dig through. He pushed his hand in as far as he could, and to his surprise it punched out into air on the other end.

He threw himself against the cold wall, and it gave way.

Within seconds he stood in the valley where the Valley People lived. He was not far from the quaint village where his loyal subjects had brought him the chocolate crown. Those people were nowhere to be found. Now standing before him was a hostile crowd, the most hostile among them being Graham, the deposed king. He stood at the forefront, his cherry red hair glowing with rage.

"Well," Graham said, "you've come back."

Brushing what was probably ice cream from his front, Tim noticed that he again had the chocolate crown on his head—Graham's old crown.

"You're right," Tim said simply.

"Good," said Graham, his expression brightening. "I've been reinstated as king, and you have my crown."

"I was given the crown by my loyal supporters."

"And it shall always be yours. You just won't wear it again. I have another that's being made." Graham turned to a number of soldierly looking men and said, "Take the crown."

They did just that, and when Tim moved to protest, two other men leaped from the crowd and pinned his arms to his sides.

The crown was removed from Tim's head. "Put it on the moose head," Graham ordered.

A strange order, Tim thought, until he saw an ornately carved totem pole nearby. About eight feet off the ground, the third head up, a goofy looking moose head was carved, its puffy nose protruding from massive antlers. The man who had removed the crown from Tim's head hooked it on the antlers. Now it hung there as if waiting to be rescued.

Suddenly everything around him froze in place—no one blinked, except for one guy caught in the act of blinking and whose eyes remained shut. Even a bird stopped, suspended in the sky.

On the totem pole just above the moose was a carving of an ugly witch doctor with a round, frowning face and hook nose. To Tim's amazement the witch doctor spoke! "Retrieve your crown by the time the sun sets over the fruitcake dam, and you will find what you seek."

The instant the last word died on the witch doctor's lips, everything came to life again.

"Okay, put him with the others," Graham ordered with a sweep of his hand.

Hands grabbed Tim's aching shoulders and pulled him toward the village.

The others Graham referred to were Sonya and Wheaters. They stared at Tim as he was tossed through the opened doorway. Both groaned as he fell on the floor of the hut before them.

"We knew it would only be a matter of time," Wheaters said. "Graham has this jealous streak, and he was definitely jealous when she offered you that crown."

"M'name's Sonya," Sonya told him. Her injured leg was no longer injured.

"I gotta get my crown back," Tim said, getting to his feet.

"Well," said Sonya, "it's good to see you too."

"No. It's important," he told her again. "I told you back on the Rock World that I was after something."

"Oh, yes, the monster."

"Monster?" said Wheaters in alarm.

"Easy, Wheaters," Tim said. "He exploded."

"Probably drank fizzy-water," Wheaters mumbled.

Tim went to the door and found it guarded by four very large men. "Graham didn't seem so cruel before."

"I believe he's made a deal with the Mountain People," Wheaters said.

"I need to get my crown back. How long before the sun sets over the dam?"

Wheaters squinted as if thinking. "It's morning—it'll be a while yet."

"Will you help me?" Tim pleaded with them both.

But they didn't have time to answer. A muscular Valley Person appeared at the door. He held a long, black whip in one hand and fondled it lovingly with the other.

"Oh, no," said Wheaters. "Will Graham's cruelty never stop?"

"I've come for him," Muscles said, indicating Tim.

"Oh, well, then," Wheaters said, "that's okay."

"What's going on?" Tim asked, concerned.

"Just a little beating for you," Wheaters said. "You're going to be 'licoriced.' After they beat you with it, they make you eat it—that is, if you live."

CHAPTER 12

Kelly found herself alone in the milk barn at about six-thirty. But only for a few minutes. Gar joined her. Although his eyes were a little bloodshot and he yawned frequently, he was ready to help in the milking.

"Where's Tim?" Gar asked. "I've barely had a chance to talk to him."

"I don't know," Kelly replied. "It happens now and then, so we just cover for each other." But she knew it didn't happen now and then, and they never covered for each other. The last thing she wanted to look like to Gar was a snitch, so she just started working.

But when Tim didn't show up by the time they were ready to start hooking up the cows to the milking machine, Kelly asked Gar if he would check on Tim.

A few minutes later Gar returned. "He's not in his room. Mr. Donnelly, the Secret Service man, said that he went out a little after midnight and didn't come back."

"Midnight?" Kelly repeated. "He didn't waste any time. The minute Saturday was over he went to VR."

"Should we tell your father?"

"Dad'll find out soon enough. Let's get the milking done, then we can go see what he's doing. Dad'll kill him." She was exaggerating, but not by much. VR would probably be history for Tim.

"Could he have fallen asleep in there or something?" Gar asked.

"Could be. But right now we have the cows to do. We'll see what kind of trouble he's gotten himself into later."

When the milking was done and the last bit of equipment cleaned, Kelly and Gar emerged from the milk barn looking for her father. The only sign of him was the telltale sound of a tractor growling off in the soybean field. "Dad must be falling behind—trying to get a little work in before church. Maybe Tim will get away with this," Kelly said to Gar. "Let's go over to my uncle's and get Tim back here. Church doesn't start for an hour and a half, so there's still time to get him and get back. I hope he remembers this when *I* goof up."

Followed by one of the Secret Service agents, Kelly and Gar made their way across the fields to Uncle Morty's.

Although Uncle Morty did milk Elvira every morning, Sunday was a late morning for Elvira. Uncle Morty didn't get up until seven or seven-thirty. Which meant that when Kelly and Gar got there at eight-thirty, Uncle Morty was just finishing up.

"A little early, isn't it?" he asked, yawning.

"Is Tim in VR?" Kelly asked.

"Don't know. Go in and see."

They did, and he was. It did look like he was sleeping in the black suit. It reclined slightly, and Tim was curled up as if he thought he was on a firm surface. But that's not all they saw. A message flashed on the large screen above the keyboard console. "Kelly or Uncle Morty; I need help. It'll only take a few minutes, but I need you to come in and give me a hand."

The Secret Service agent was now standing at the computer room door, and when he read the message, he muttered under his breath, "Don't even think it."

Gar ignored him. "Want to go in and see what it's all about?"

"Both of us?"

"Sure. I've been in there before, even if it wasn't that much fun. This time it'll be different."

"It can get a little strange in there," Kelly said remembering the lightning and her close call.

"Tim's probably just trying to debug something—maybe trying to correct a programming error—and he needs some help. Come on. We'll help him and get out. He probably fell asleep working on it. You know how programming can be. You work and work and miss the obvious."

"With me I work and work and nearly get hit by lightning."

Gar walked toward the black suits.

"Gar, I don't think the president would approve," the Secret Service agent said.

"It'll only be for a couple of minutes, and if it's longer I'll come out."

"You sure?" the agent asked to extract a commitment.

"Sure," replied Gar. "Come on. I've always wanted to get back in there."

Kelly shrugged. "Well, at least there's no bad guys around this time."

The Secret Service agent still wasn't convinced, but he also found it hard to come up with a good reason why not. After all, what he'd been told about VR was that it was little more than a super-sophisticated video game. And how could a video game hurt anyone? "I'll be right out here if you need me."

Within a minute or two Kelly was zipping up her black suit and watching Gar do the same.

She was actually looking forward to this. Maybe there would be a chance to show Gar what she had done. She could show him her invention that created amusement park rides—even introduce him to the White Knight. She swallowed hard. Maybe she wouldn't introduce him to the White Knight. Maybe she'd turn the White Knight into an amusement park ride. All she needed was for Gar to see who the White Knight was.

Monitoring Tim while he slept in VR, Hammond Helbert listened, by way of the small mike he'd planted next to the VR machine, to the conversation that was taking place in the computer room. He was elated. His plan was beginning to unfold just as he thought it would. In fact, the president's son would be an added bonus. But there was no time to gloat. He had things to do.

Both visors came down at the same moment, and both ignited with picture-perfect animation. Kelly recognized the place right away. They stood in their Robin Hood-type costumes—she in her richly designed sky blue dress, Gar in forest green pants and shirt—on the grass just outside her castle.

Gar looked cute in his Robin Hood suit. On his back was a quiver of arrows, and lashed across his chest was the string of a bow.

Kelly was a little surprised that they had entered her virtual land on the front lawn. She had only created one entry point, the golden end of the rainbow, which was the way she had always come in before.

But not only did they stand on the emerald front lawn, they also stood at the entrance to the parachute ride her invention had conjured up. The last time she'd gone up with Sir Edwin and had come down to find the Crimson Knight waiting for her. What would happen this time?

"There's a note on the inside of the parachute basket," Gar pointed out.

Pinned to the basket, the one that would carry them aloft, was a piece of paper with something printed on it. After snatching it, Kelly read it aloud:

> Kelly,
>
> I'm on to something. An incredible discovery hidden in VR somewhere. But you can't leave VR until I've found it. If you leave, all the doors close—whatever they are—and we'll never find it. It's something Matthew Helbert did, and it's worth millions—everything he does is worth millions. Find me. I need your help—I keep getting hurt. There will be notes along the way telling you what to do. Remember, stay in VR, no matter what. And don't stop until you find me.
>
> Tim.

"Dad's going to love this," Gar muttered darkly.

"Both our dads," Kelly agreed. "But, although it pains me to say it, Tim usually knows what he's talking about."

"Matthew Helbert's the developer of this VR machine, isn't he?"

"He went to school with my uncle. They're both geniuses. Uncle Morty went to work for the government, and Matthew started inventing things. If it is something Matthew Helbert did, it will be worth millions. But more important, because he's a Christian now, you know, it'll probably help people."

"So what do we do?" Gar asked, looking around. To his amazement, a brightly colored parrot flew out of the nearby woods and landed on his shoulder. "My cockatiel back at the White House won't even do that," he said a little nervously.

Before Kelly could comment, the parrot squawked, then said quite clearly, "Take a ride. Take a ride." It flapped its red, blue, and yellow wings and flew back into the woods.

"Well, that was clear enough," Kelly said. "You like parachute rides?"

"When they work."

"This one should," Kelly said, patting her pocket and feeling her TV remote-sized invention there. "I built it myself."

"Before we drop to our doom here, shouldn't we at least try to tell someone in the real world what's going on?"

Kelly nodded. "Message: console," she said in clear tones. The communications monitor responded by placing the message "Enter" on the lower right corner of her visor.

"Dad or Uncle Morty: Matthew Helbert's got a treasure that Tim's trying to find. If we leave VR, we won't ever be able to find it again. Uncle Morty, maybe you could come in and help too. That way we can get out of here faster. Tim says to try and find him and not to stop until you do. This is Kelly."

Unknown to Kelly, Hammond Helbert intercepted the message and rewrote it. The message that blinked on the console now read, "Uncle Morty. We need help. Tim's on the trail of something very big. It'll only take a few minutes. Come in as soon as you can. Kelly."

The message sent, Kelly and Gar climbed aboard the parachute gondola. "Hold on," Kelly said, but she didn't have to. Gar was already holding on.

The moment the gate on the gondola closed, the parachute began to rise. Just as before, the higher it got, the more nervous Kelly became. Unlike before, Gar was there to see it. So not only was she nervous and shrinking against the sides of the basket, but she was turning the deepest ruby red as well.

"You okay?" Gar asked when they were about three-quarters of the way up.

"I hate heights. Airplanes give me heart attacks."

"I don't like heights either," he confided and placed a reassuring hand on hers.

They came to the top and hung there suspended for a moment.

"What now?" Gar asked.

"Now we—" They dropped.

The parachute above them billowed as it met the air resistance and then began to drift. There was a major difference this time, however. Before, when Kelly and Sir Edwin had dropped beneath the parachute, the guide wires had kept them in line as they descended to the ground.

Now there were no guide wires. They had disappeared.

"Oh, no," Kelly whimpered. She was desperately trying to keep her composure in front of Gar, but her efforts failed. Not only was she plastered against the side of the gondola—now she was beginning to shake. They were in free fall, as if dropped from a plane—something else Kelly didn't want to think about. But they were drifting on a current of air heading away from the castle grounds toward the forest and the unknown beyond it.

"We're okay," Gar said, moving toward her.

"Don't move," Kelly gasped. "You might upset something."

"I was trying to keep *you* from being upset."

"Just don't move. It shakes when you move."

Gar nodded and turned his attention to the scene below—the castle in the distance falling even further away, the deep green forest surrounding everything, a naked hill off in the distance with a splintered, burned tree at its crest. All of it sprawled out below them. Even though Kelly was scared to death, Gar found it all exciting and wondered where they were going. "It doesn't seem like we're dropping," he finally said.

Kelly instantly turned green. "We're flying?! Even a plane's better than a parachute at flying."

"There's something over the horizon," Gar said, moving to the gondola's edge and peering at it.

Kelly found it hard to care, but she did straighten herself a little so that she could see.

"Mountains," Gar said.

Kelly forgot a little of her fear as she looked toward the horizon.

They were mountains, great ranges of them. Though still quite distant, they appeared white with smudges of brown, particularly at their summits, with clouds that looked like heaps of whipped cream.

"We're moving faster," Gar said.

It was not what she wanted to hear—faster meant crashing into something even harder.

Below them, the forest ended and the distant mountain, now far less distant, grew. Soon they were gliding through a high mountain pass. Below lay a snow field; on either side rose tall cliffs, the cliffs on the left looking like piles of scooped ice cream, on the right like sleek ski slopes. Everything was white, except for one rich brown river cascading down the piled scoops and a ruby red one oozing from an even taller summit. Both finally disappeared from view as they headed further down the mountain.

Something struck the gondola hard. Kelly's heart leaped to her throat as the basket shuddered under the impact.

"What was that?" Kelly gasped.

Something else fired by.

"A big bullet of some kind," Gar said, eyes glued to the left cliff. Somewhere in those scoops someone seemed to be firing at them.

Another and another streaked by. Then one hit the gondola again. Instinctively, Gar placed himself between Kelly and the sniper.

Several big bullets in rapid succession struck all around them; some hit the gondola; some hit Gar. He winced in sudden pain. It was as if he'd been punched twice in the chest and arm.

"You okay?" Kelly asked.

"Now that hurt."

"A peanut," Kelly said as she saw the roasted nut lying on the gondola floor. "They're shooting nuts at us. Big nuts." That they were; although there was no doubt that they were peanuts, each was about the size of an elongated orange.

Another volley, this one aimed at the parachute. Several struck it and tore a gaping hole on the forward edge. They began to drop.

"I hate when that happens," Kelly exclaimed.

"Out there," Gar shouted. "I see the gun."

Now Kelly did too—a large, orange-sized barrel protruding from beneath an upside down triangle where the peanuts were apparently stored. The marksman aimed the barrel then cranked a handle on the side. Peanuts rifled out of the barrel, the volley tearing an even greater hole in the parachute.

"We're going to crash!" Kelly cried.

To protect her, Gar pushed her down and toward the back of the gondola, the part that would likely hit last, then huddled over her.

Seconds later they hit.

But it was a squishy impact. The gondola struck ground, plowed into the snowfield's surface, then was dragged several feet before the parachute collapsed on top of them.

"That wasn't so bad," Gar said, remaining crouched beneath the parachute canopy.

Kelly was a little overwhelmed by Gar's selflessness. He'd protected her a number of times already. "Thank you," she said gratefully.

"That's okay, but we'd better get going. If they'd shoot us out of the sky, they won't be welcoming us now. We'd better get out of here."

But that idea fizzled when the parachute was pulled away from above them, and an ugly round face took its place. "You Valley People think you can escape from us in something like this? Come, we'll show you what we do to Valley People. How'd you like to become a chocolate dip?"

Kelly said she'd rather not, but the ugly round face insisted.

Hammond Helbert loved what was happening. The Kelly-girl and Gar would soon be hurting, and the Tim-guy was already hurting. Any minute now that troublesome Morty-character would read the message on the console and enter VR, and then they'd all be hooked by their greed and desire to make themselves important.

Hammond Helbert laughed.

He had given Tim the beating himself. Although one of the guards had taken Tim to the place of punishment, it was Hammond Helbert himself, disguised in the furry white clothing of the Valley People, who used the black licorice whip on Tim. The black VR suit simulated it well. He'd improved that part of the programming himself when the CIA had had the machine for that short time. But not only was he proud of the programming he'd done, it felt good to begin exacting his revenge. It was all he could do to keep from cheering. But he'd stopped after ten strokes. He didn't want Tim so upset that he would decide to leave VR. Revenge would be coming in much stronger doses later.

Tim woke slowly. His shoulders and back still stung. He couldn't believe he'd actually endured it. He also couldn't believe that Matthew had programmed such a thing for anyone. Was it an initiation or something? Did Matthew want him to earn whatever it was he sought?

How long had he been asleep? He didn't know. The sun was high overhead now and would probably start its descent soon. He had to get that crown before the sun dropped behind the fruitcake dam.

He saw Wheaters and Sonya sitting on the floor leaning against the hut wall. They turned his way as he rolled over and sat up.

"Good, you're awake," Wheaters said.

"How are your wounds?" Sonya asked, moving over to him.

"They hurt."

"Don't think about that now," Wheaters said with a sense of urgency. "We have to escape."

"I have to get my crown back."

"Always politics."

"It's got nothing to do with politics. I need it before sunset."

"Politics or not, it doesn't matter. You have only two choices. Get the crown, or escape from that dam and the billion tons of chocolate behind it. Time won't let you have both. And the chocolate's hot too. There's an underground hot spring beneath it."

"But didn't you say that Graham made a pact with the Mountain People?"

"They'll betray him. They always do. He's just bitter because his own people have rejected him, so he's chosen to forget the treachery of the Mountain People. They are pumping up the cherries with fizzy-water as we speak. They want to wipe us out. Always have. They won't let any agreement stand in their way. It'll just make it easier to catch us off guard. In the meantime they'll give Graham enough cherry launchers and peanut guns to keep the dissenters in line—those who crowned you." He indicated Sonya. "They've been dissatisfied for years and were looking desperately for a messiah. You fit the bill."

"But the crown?"

"Forget the crown for now. Escape is our only option."

"He's right, sweet Tim," Sonya said, her almond eyes big and pleading.

"Okay, how?"

Wheaters tapped his foot on the floor. "We get through the flooring, then dig our way to freedom."

Looking at a floor made from what appeared to be some pretty thick planks, Tim asked, "How do we get through that?"

Wheaters only smiled. He bent down and easily lifted one. "We haven't perfected our prisons yet."

"But why didn't you escape already?"

"I'm cranky, but I'm not all that smart. I just thought of it myself."

◫

High above Tim and Sonya, Kelly and Gar stood before their captors—six men and women who sat sternly at a long table. They had heard the guards' description of Kelly and Gar's landing and now were trying to decide what to do. After all, the intruders were obviously spies sent by the Valley People. So far, the two proposals on the table were to bury them in ice cream and let them freeze to death or smother them by hanging them by their ankles and dipping them in chocolate.

Neither suggestion thrilled Kelly and Gar, but they didn't seem to have a vote. After a few minutes of more discussion, dipping them in chocolate won.

The Dipper, as they had heard it called, was little more than a gallows that extended out over a broad lake of chocolate. In the cold air generated by the ice cream mountains, steam rose from the warm chocolate's surface. The chocolate ripples lapped and hardened at the ice cream shore.

"How far do you think all this will go?" Gar asked Kelly as they were being led from the court to the gallows.

"I don't know. I didn't program any of this."

"Stop talking!" a bulldog-faced guard shouted. "The condemned are not allowed to talk."

"I hate being condemned," Kelly muttered. "And there's no reason to stay that way."

She saw an opportunity to escape. Part of the path to the lake bordered a steep incline, one that dropped for a long way. There was a small safety fence at that point, but she could easily jump it. If she and Gar survived the steep drop, they would have a good head start on anyone following. And she was sure that no one would follow. The incline was so steep that you'd have to be an idiot to jump down it in the first place.

There was no way to tell Gar her plan. She'd just have to hope he followed her lead.

The safety fence was coming up. She glanced back at Gar, then, when the walkway and the incline met, she dove over the side. Gar, at first bewildered, finally realized what she was doing and dove after her.

It *was* steep, almost a sheer drop. But the drop was only part of the problem. Instead of a sleek ski slope like other parts of the mountain, this one was dotted by thick chunks of hard chocolate—rocks that protruded from the mountainside. As they slid and ran and fell, they frequently slammed into the hard chocolate, bruising themselves. At least there were no trees to avoid, but the chunks of chocolate made the lack of trees a small benefit.

They kept falling. And as they did they screamed when shocked and groaned when hurt. They did both a lot. They tumbled and rolled. They were cold too—very cold. Their hands were aching, ice cream had gotten down their fronts and backs and into their shoes. All in all, it was not a fun trip.

The bottom has to be coming up, Kelly thought hopefully. *It just has to.*

That's when she slammed against a particularly large mass of chocolate, bending her back and knocking the wind out of her. Just behind her, Gar saw a glimpse of what happened and grabbed at anything to stop his descent so he could help, but he couldn't stop. He crashed into his own massive boulder of chocolate below Kelly.

Plastered against the rock, Gar called up to her, "You okay?"

"My back," she gasped. "I can hardly breathe."

Gar propped himself against the boulder and tried to figure out how he might get up to her, but the face of the slope was too slick. There was no way to go up and only one way down.

Something flew by and buried itself in the ice cream. "An arrow," Gar said in disbelief. "They don't use arrows."

"Oh, no," groaned Kelly. From her vantage point, still at least thirty feet from the bottom of the slope, the identity of the archer below them became clear as glass. "The Crimson Knight," she muttered. "What's he doing here?"

Another arrow *thwanged* and stuck in the chocolate block that had stopped her descent.

"Who's he?" Gar called up to her.

"Who am I?" came the Crimson Knight's bellow. "I'm the one with a score to settle."

From above them came a volley of peanuts. They rained down on them, slapping at the chocolate rocks and digging into the hillside. Kelly looked up to see the barrel of a peanut gun pointing right down the slope. Though they were reasonably protected from the knight's arrows by the chocolate boulders, the peanut gun had a clear shot at them.

No way down; no way up. Kelly and Gar were trapped.

CHAPTER 13

Sonya did *not* like crawling through cake.

"Mice do this," she said. "Not me."

But she did it anyway.

Wheaters led the way. After lifting a few planks, he all but dove into the soft valley floor. Sonya then eased herself into the hole that Wheaters had made, and then, finally, Tim followed Sonya. But before he did, he put the planks back in place to hide their escape route.

In a single file, the three kept digging.

"Where are we going?" Sonya finally asked after they'd been at it for a while.

"As far away from the village as possible; then we'll stop and decide where to go next," Wheaters said, his feet kicking cake into Sonya's face.

"I'll make that decision now," Tim called up to him.

"Where?" Sonya asked, her hair covered in crumbs.

"Head for the fizzy-water," Tim said firmly.

"Really?" Wheaters said, with an appreciative hum.

The peanut guns above them pinned Kelly and Gar down and occasionally hit their mark. Kelly's upper arms were bruised from being struck, and Gar's thighs had taken a couple of hits in succession.

"It's like dodgeball," Gar called up to her. "Only the balls are harder and come faster." Another one ricocheted off his knee cap. He collapsed with a painful shudder.

"You hit?" said Kelly. "You okay?"

"I think the next time you ask me out on a virtual date, I'll refuse."

Although she hated the idea of Gar getting hurt, she couldn't help asking, "Is this a date?"

"It can't be. I'm not supposed to date."

"Me neither," Kelly said. "But if it were a date would you have gone with me?"

"Sure. But the next time I see peanuts I want to see elephants eating them."

"Come down, you cowards," the Crimson Knight called up again. It was a recurring theme for him. He'd said it several times. He wanted to get on with things too. Some of the peanuts from above were hitting him as well.

An explosion occurred above them. Something had struck the mountain slope.

"One of those cherries!" cried Kelly.

"They're being fired from the other side," Gar cried back.

The mountain heaved a bone-jarring quake. A huge wave of ice cream broke loose and, like an avalanche, slid toward them in a wave.

With little time to react, her back still aching, Kelly did the only thing she could. She spun away from the chocolate boulder and raced the ice cream wave toward the bottom of the mountain.

Seeing Kelly act, Gar leaped out from behind his chocolate rock and fell in beside her. Now they both charged toward the base of the mountain and the Crimson Knight waiting there.

But he, too, had seen the ice cream wave and pulled back. Another red cherry slammed into the ice cream mountain and exploded. This one created another wave that followed the first. Neither Kelly nor Gar saw the second bomb hit, but they did see the resulting wall of ice cream.

It was right on their tails.

Frantic to get out of the way, they dove and rolled and tumbled, ice cream covering and freezing them. And all the way they screamed, screams forced to the surface by the adrenalin boiling within.

They reached the base of the mountain, the wave lapping at their heels, but they didn't stop. Although their feet sloshed and sank deep into the ice cream, they couldn't stop. Not yet. The wave was billowing right behind them. Soon they'd outrun it, but they still weren't safe. They heard the distant cries of the Mountain People in pursuit.

Suddenly the Crimson Knight, red and mighty against the white background, stood like a tower before them, a sharp lance extending from his arm to a point about chest high — where their hearts thundered.

"Hello, milady," the knight said.

"What are you doing here?" Kelly challenged. "You're supposed to be—"

"I've come for you."

"Try lightning around here," Kelly said defiantly, "and everything melts. The mountain will swallow you up."

"I've learned, milady," said the red menace looking through his grilled visor.

"Who is this guy?" Gar asked.

"He wants to fry me."

"Why?"

"I burned his house down—lightning. With this thing I invented."

"I like to invent things too."

"Really? Like what?"

"Like a little thing to put my mouse away in."

"Computer mouse?"

"It's like a little hook thing."

"I haven't invented anything on the outside yet."

"Stop!" the Crimson Knight exploded. When Kelly and Gar gave him their attention, he calmed but still waved the point of the lance between their two hearts. "There's a pool near here. What goes in never comes out. It will be your new home."

"What if we don't want to go?" Kelly said.

"Then I drive this right through your heart," said the Crimson Knight with such sincerity that Kelly's heart acknowledged the threat by missing several beats. "Move," the knight said, indicating the direction with the point of his lance. "It's just over there."

▣

"I can't believe we're breathing air again," Sonya finally said, her head poking up above the ground like a golf ball on a tee. "Do you know what crumbs can do to a hairdo?"

Two other heads were teed up beside her.

They had surfaced on the valley floor just where the fruitcake dam and the sleek ice cream mountain met. Tim saw a trail leading up the edge of the dam into the mountains.

"Where's the fizzy-water from here?" Tim asked.

"There are two springs of it," Wheaters said. He turned to the far end of the valley. "The one up there is out of reach. There's another that's high atop the mountain, about where that cookie comes out."

Tim didn't hesitate. "Let's go."

The pool the Crimson Knight referred to was a rich ruby red and bubbled at its center, maybe as a result of being fed from an underground spring. One edge of the pool was lower, and the ruby substance oozed over the edge, waves and waves of it falling to the valley below. It looked incredibly gooey.

Kelly and Gar walked before the knight's lance but neither sensed doom. Something had to happen—it always did, especially when they both prayed. The Lord wouldn't let them drown in strawberry topping.

But the pool was getting awfully close, and they weren't in the best condition to swim—Gar's knee still ached; he walked with a slight limp, and Kelly's arms burned from where they'd been struck repeatedly by the peanuts.

As they approached the pool, they both looked around to see where their deliverance might come from. But by the time they reached the edge of the pool, it still hadn't come.

They stood at the end of the lance, their toes hanging over the edge.

"Who will jump first?"

Gar turned to Kelly and Kelly to Gar.

Kelly felt the lance jab her back. It was sharp, and it hurt.

She watched the bubbling surface. Was it hot like the chocolate?

"Who's first?" the knight asked insistently.

Sloshy hoofbeats came from somewhere behind them, splattering, driving louder, robbed of their thunder but wild and frightening.

Kelly felt the lance pull away, and she turned. Gar turned too. It was the White Knight. The Crimson Knight had pulled around and was facing their oncoming savior. He approached at a wildly pulsing pace, his lance down, ready for battle.

"This'll be good," Gar said, his voice excited.

It was good—and it was quick.

Like the meeting of two locomotives, the white and red slammed together. Horses' chests flattened against each other. They cried in frantic whinnies. Lances struck together; red and white blurred as the knights were unseated, tangled chaotically, and fell to wallow in the ice creamed earth.

The frightened horses pranced and twirled, reared and cried, their hooves dodging, then battering each other in a blur of activity.

The Crimson Knight finally got to his feet, but when he rose both Kelly and Gar saw that this would be the Crimson Knight's last charge. The White Knight's lance had broken, and the last three feet of it were now lodged in the Crimson Knight's midsection. The White Knight, maybe to ease his opponent's pain, grabbed the protruding end and gave it a pull. He then dropped the blood-stained weapon to the ground. The Crimson Knight collapsed next to it.

But the horses were still dealing violently with each other, and Kelly and Gar were having a hard time keeping away from the edge of the pool. When they went one way, the horses intruded. When they went the other, the same thing. The horses seemed to be continuing the battle their riders had already finished.

"Are you all right?" the White Knight called out to them as he removed his helmet.

As he spoke, the horses spun around again. This time the one draped in crimson struck Kelly. She tried in vain to recapture her balance, but she slipped into the gooey pool.

Gar quickly dropped to his knees to offer a hand to Kelly when she resurfaced.

But she didn't.

Maybe the knight was right. Maybe when you went into the pool you didn't come back out. "Kelly!" he cried. But he knew his cry was useless. There was only one thing to do. He stood, said a two-word prayer, "Jesus, help!" and dove into the goo.

Tim and Wheaters found the climb difficult. Sonya found it

all but impossible. She didn't like hard tasks. Her life needed to be fun or not at all. She chose "not at all" several times, but never went through with her threat "not to take another step." Being left alone to be captured by either the Valley People or the Mountain People was worse than climbing up ice cream. Climbing up the cookie that cut the mountain was difficult, but a little better. Her complaints came less frequently.

They were making progress. The valley and the village sprawled below, the chocolate river snaking through it. The dam looked smaller, and from their position they could see some of the chocolate reservoir, the steam from the heat wisping up from the surface.

"How much further?" Tim asked, eyeing the sun's progress. He had a couple of hours left, but he was still very far away. He wondered if the crown still hung from that moose's head.

Wheaters didn't reply but put his finger to his lips. He motioned that the fizzy-water was just over the next rise. He pulled Tim closer. "There'll be guards."

"What's going on?" Sonya asked.

"Shhh," Wheaters told her.

"Stay here," Tim whispered, "I'm going to take a look."

A moment later, he lay on a patch of hard chocolate on the crest of the little rise and watched the operation unfolding below. Just above the cookie was a pool of water—it fizzed like soda water, minute bubbles leaping from its surface like a fog. It fizzed so loudly that he could hear it from where he lay. A red licorice rope ran from the pool to a pump. Two fur-clad men pumped it. Another red licorice rope led from the pump to a syringe. A pile of the basketball-sized red cherries was next, before which stood a guy holding the syringe. Another worker took a cherry from the pile, the syringe guy stabbed it with the syringe and told the pumpers to pump until the cherry was full of fizzy-water, then he requested another cherry and repeated the process.

As the cherries were filled, they were loaded onto a conveyor that took them down the rise to a distant catapult. It wasn't a high-tech facility, and the catapult wasn't a cannon, but Tim had a feeling it did the job. And soon it would do the job *he* wanted done.

As Wheaters had suggested, there was a guard. On a raised platform not far from the cherry injection station rested a peanut gun and a fur-clad guard. He didn't look all that alert, but, then, he didn't have to. If anyone charged him, he or she would have to run across a wide open area, giving the guard plenty of time to react and blast away.

Okay, Tim knew what he wanted to do.

But how was he going to do it?

🔲

The instant Kelly dropped into the strawberry topping, she knew she was in trouble. She just sank. In water the air in her body would have buoyed her back to the surface. But with this stuff, she might as well have had lead in her lungs.

As she sank, she grabbed for the side of the pool. But when she touched it, it was slick. She just kept dropping. She tried to swim—kick her feet and work her arms—but if she made progress, she never knew it.

And all the time, she couldn't breathe.

There was an odor—the wonderfully pungent odor of strawberries—but no air to go along with it. Her lungs, crying for air, now seemed ready to collapse.

She felt something. Her hand found it, and it moved and found her back. Gar? She could only see red, but he was pulling her. To the surface? She didn't know where the surface was. She decided just to trust him.

No air. She grabbed at air, her lungs pulled in, but there was nothing to pull. She had to change the VR suit—put at least a little hole in it so this would never happen again. If she lived.

She did.

A moment later, just when she knew it was over, Gar gave another strong pull, and her head broke free of the strawberry topping. She took a huge, rejuvenating breath and then remained there panting. Only after air was returned to every cell in her body did she notice her surroundings. She was at the summit of the falls. But it wasn't really a fall; it was more like an incredibly steep slope, just like the one they had come down, only steeper. The strawberry topping oozed around her neck on its way down a long descent.

"Ready?" Gar asked.

Hair caked with strawberry topping, her face still sticky with it, Kelly eyed him with questioning brows. "For what?"

"To ride it down. There's a village down there."

"There's perfectly solid ground up here too."

"There's bad guys up here."

"But—I don't know if I want to drop three miles straight down."

"Sure, you do. It's the fastest way off this mountain, and the people up here want to kill us."

Kelly eyed the long descent again. He was right. The Mountain People still wanted to turn them into a chocolate dip. Smothering in strawberry topping had been bad enough. "Well, okay."

"I gotta ask you something first, though."

"What?"

"That White Knight back there—he looked like me."

"Really?" Kelly said, trying to sound nonchalant while she contemplated the very long drop.

"I thought I wasn't seeing what I was seeing, but the more I thought about it the more I knew I really was seeing it."

"You sure are a guy with words."

"Was it me?"

"Maybe the computer had your picture somewhere. Come on, if we're going to do this, let's do it."

Kelly pushed herself out of the strawberry topping, sat for a moment on the edge of the slope, the topping oozing all around her. Gar did the same, and for an instant they sat together.

"Hey," came a charged voice, "there they are." A peanut slammed into the topping just in back of them. Another whizzed past Gar's head; another whizzed past Kelly's.

Concerned that Gar might get the wrong—well, right—impression about why the White Knight looked like him, Kelly felt compelled to speak. "Before we go, I have to say something—"

But Gar didn't wait. "No time. Let's go!" They launched themselves off the edge. Instantly they were engulfed by and cushioned on top of the goo as it slid down the slick ice cream mountain.

Tim, Sonya, and Wheaters lay on the patch of hard chocolate on the summit of the small rise. It was time to act. The sun was creeping relentlessly toward the horizon beyond the dam, and unless Tim got the crown back all would be lost. Plus, there was no reason to wait. Nothing would improve if they did. So Tim brought them all to this vantage point to show them what he had planned.

"I need to capture that peanut gun, and the only way to do that is to make the gunner up there concentrate on something else while I run across that area and climb up there."

"A diversion. Yes." Wheaters understood.

"Good. Wheaters, I want you to run along that ridge over there." Tim pointed toward a long raised area on the opposite side of the fizzy-water injection compound. It ran high and flat for at least a hundred yards then reached the mountain and stopped. "You can crawl out of sight behind the ridge, then when you get there, leap up and start running. When he fires at you, I'll run to the base of the tower and climb up the ladder."

"When he fires at me?" Wheaters clearly didn't like that part.

"Sure. But those peanuts hurt only a little."

"Even a little is too much."

"But we have to get the gun, and that's our only hope."

"*You* have to get the gun. I'm on high ground now. When they destroy the dam with all those cherry bombs, I won't be bothered in the slightest now."

"But your people will be drowned," Tim argued.

"That's their problem. I'm safe now. I don't intend to get shot at—even if it only hurts a little."

"But—"

"I'll do it," Sonya said, her eyes fixed on the distant ridge.

"You will?" Tim said, remembering her complaining on the way up.

"It's what *you* want," she said matter-of-factly.

"But you might get hurt."

"You didn't care if I got hurt," Wheaters protested.

"Are you sure?" Tim questioned Sonya, ignoring Wheaters's point.

"Give me a few minutes to get over there. When I pop up and he starts firing, do your thing," she answered.

"Well," Tim began reluctantly, "okay. You be careful and just draw his fire; don't present too good a target."

She smiled a distant, frightened little smile and then crawled off.

When Kelly said it to herself, sliding down a steep ice cream slope on a bed of strawberry topping sounded like fun. It wasn't. At least not for her. Even though she rested on a bed of goo, a bed that conformed to her every contour and was actually comfortable, she was moving far too fast—far too fast to even fool herself into believing she was in control.

Fortunately, she wasn't going anywhere that could hurt her—yet.

Gar was a little ahead of her. She could hear him calling back to her now and then, but she had no idea what he was saying. His voice was the only indistinguishable sound rising above the rush of air in her ears. Anyway, her heart was thundering too loudly for her to hear anything else but that.

After the first few minutes, though, even for all the speed, Kelly actually found herself relaxing a little. Of course, she began to relax just as everything changed.

She saw Gar rise above the ruby goo and fly off, propelled by his own speed, excess goo dripping from him as he flew. As it turned out, he hadn't risen above the goo, the goo had dropped from beneath him—as it now did to her.

They'd come to a goo-fall, a ledge over which the strawberry topping gushed.

Kelly screamed as she plunged feetfirst toward a white clearing below.

Gar hit first—*shlark!* He hit the ground like a spear and was buried to his knees. Kelly did the same. Being a little lighter, she was buried only to her ankles.

Kelly, still stunned to be alive after her fall, allowed her knees to collapse. She sat on the ice cream floor.

"You okay?" Gar asked, climbing out of the hole his legs had made.

"I think that at my next birthday I'll just have cake."

"Let me help you out."

"No, I want to sit here for a minute. We're not moving anywhere now, are we? We are standing still?"

"For now. That village is a little closer."

"It better be a lot closer," Kelly said, eyeing Gar, who decided to rest on a chocolate boulder. But the moment he planted himself there, his expression changed. His brows knit, his eyes became questioning. He was seeing something that puzzled him. "Look," he said, pointing off toward the other end of the valley. "He's sailing over the village."

Kelly followed Gar's finger. A man sailed into the ice cream world just as they had—in the gondola of a parachute.

"They're shooting at him," Kelly cried.

They were. From the cliffs on either side, peanut guns fired away. Kelly and Gar could see the peanuts flying past, some hitting the gondola and bouncing off. The man in it ducked but kept his head up so that he could see where he was going. Several cherry bombs flew from the far cliff. One struck the gondola and exploded. It tore a gaping hole in the gondola. The man braced himself and stared at the hole.

"He's got a problem," Kelly said. "That basket can't hold together much longer. I wonder who it is."

Kelly was right. The moment she said it the floor of the gondola gave way, and they saw the man's legs drop through the bottom. He looked like he was going to fall, but he held on. As the parachute sailed across the valley, he hung there, knowing undoubtedly that if he lost his grip it would all be over.

Now the peanut guns had something more interesting to shoot at. Maybe that made for a better target, because they were beginning to hit the man consistently. Gar and Kelly saw him trying to evade the incoming rounds but to no avail.

"He's coming this way," Gar said.

Kelly pulled her feet out of the creamy mire and walked quickly over to Gar. The drama unfolded rapidly as the man hung there and was pelted by peanuts, all the time fighting to hold his grip.

"It's Uncle Morty!" she finally said, a bolt of recognition charging through her.

"He must have seen your message."

That's when they noticed they weren't alone. Five men emerged from the surrounding chocolate boulders. Two of them took hold of Kelly and Gar while the other three, led by a guy with a cherry red beard and hair, stood watching Uncle Morty float their way. He said to the others, "We'll wait here for him." He turned to Kelly and Gar. "The Mountain People must want you three pretty bad. Maybe they'll trade something big for you."

CHAPTER 14

Tim and Wheaters lay on the rise waiting for Sonya to show herself. It had been a long time, and Tim was getting nervous. Maybe she'd been seen. But if she had then the compound would have been alerted, and there was nothing alert about this compound.

"Over there," Wheaters pointed.

Sure enough, Sonya's head was peeking over the opposite rise. She gave Tim a little wave then hesitated for a moment as if to gather courage. Courage firmly in place, she leaped to her feet and ran along the crest of the rise in full view.

As Tim expected, she got no more than a few feet before the peanut gun started blasting away at her. At first the rounds fell behind her, but within a few seconds the gunner had found his range. The peanuts started hitting home.

But Tim couldn't wait to see what happened to Sonya. The best thing he could do for her now was to move quickly. Running for all he was worth, he reached the base of the tower and began climbing the ladder. He did none of this undetected, however. The guy with the syringe saw him and yelled to the gunner. But the gunner was too busy. He had his target and was laying into her.

Tim climbed the ladder quickly and broke through the opening in the floor. The gunner crouched there behind the gun cranking away as fast as he could.

The gunner never knew what hit him. Tim took a peanut in each hand and clapped them together with the gunner's head in between. The gunner slumped to one side. Tim took only a second to see how Sonya had fared. She sat on the crest of the rise hugging her legs. Tim couldn't tell whether she was in pain or not—could a computer character feel pain? It didn't matter right now. What mattered was that he had the peanut gun, and the bad guys had the fizzy-water compound.

Tim turned the gun around and started firing at the pumpers. It didn't take much. The pumpers fled after only a few rounds. The injector stood his ground for a few minutes, but when a peanut hit a full cherry and it exploded all over him, he ran off. When he left, so did the guys who loaded the cherries on the conveyor.

Although far off, the guard for the cherry catapult went next. Finding that the peanut gun had amazing range, Tim fired until the guard fled. Sooner than he had dared to hope, everything belonged to him.

"Sonya, you okay?" he called out to her.

She didn't answer, but she shook her head.

"What's wrong?" he called.

"My ankle again. I think it's sprained—bad. It really hurts."

Tim ran down the ladder rungs and over to Sonya. She was clutching her ankle, afraid to move. He slid up beside her. "What can I do?"

"Nothing. It just hurts. I'll be okay. I just have to stay off of it for a while—then it will heal."

"Don't we have to bind it or something?"

"The program says a few days of staying off of it and I can walk again."

Tim looked up at the sun. He had maybe an hour left.

"Okay, I'm going down to the catapult. I've got to get my crown back."

"While you play war, I'm going to someplace I like—where I'll be comfortable for a while. I like to have fun. Your kind of fun keeps getting me hurt."

"Can I help you get where you're going?"

"No. I go places pretty easily. Now, go get your crown."

Tim nodded anxiously and ran down the long path to the catapult. As he had expected, it was aimed at the fruitcake dam. He loaded one of the basketball-sized cherries into the sling, sighted down what looked like an aiming stake, and pulled the rope. The catapult let fly, and the cherry streaked toward the top of the dam. It struck a few feet from the top and exploded. When the fizzy-water and cherry juice had run away, there was a deep pockmark. Fruitcake wasn't easy to destroy, but a few more well-placed cherries and the pressure from all the chocolate behind it might cause the dam to crumble.

Tim turned to the valley and called down, "Graham! You down there?"

He shouted a couple more times before receiving a reply. It was a distant voice. "Who is it?" It sounded like Graham.

"I want my crown. Run it up here in the next few minutes, and I won't blow up the dam."

"Are you sure you want to do that? Some people down here who were asking about you would surely drown with us."

"Tim," Uncle Morty called up to him. "It's me, Uncle Morty. Kelly and Gar are here with me."

Although they were far off, Tim could see the three of them surrounded by several fur-clad guards standing near the totem. Was his crown still hanging there?

"What are they doing here?" Tim muttered to himself, his brain working quickly. "I bet they'll want a piece of Matthew's treasure." But they were closer to the crown than he was—and the sun was moving rapidly toward the horizon. Maybe Uncle Morty, Kelly, and Gar could figure out a way to get the crown to him. *That would be worth ten percent—tops, though, no more. Twenty, maybe,* he thought. He glanced toward the sun again. Maybe a half hour before it died behind the dam. Then his opportunity for fame and riches would die with it.

"Kelly, Uncle Morty," Tim shouted. There were no echoes as the ice cream cliffs on either side swallowed the sound.

"We're okay," shouted Uncle Morty as if sure that question was on Tim's mind.

It wasn't. Why were they here? That was his question. Maybe God had brought them just to get the crown for him—now that was possible. "I need the crown," he called out. "On the moose. I need it before the sun goes down, or we lose everything." The "we" was calculated. Now they knew he'd share with them—but they didn't know how much.

Down below, Kelly looked around. "Moose? What moose?"

"What's this all about?" Uncle Morty called up to him.

"Don't know. But it's big," came Tim's reply.

"That's enough," one of the guards growled. "No more talking."

Kelly finally spotted the moose head on the totem and the

chocolate crown hanging on it. She nudged Gar and Uncle Morty. When they turned, she pointed at it. "Over there."

"Why would he want that?" Gar asked.

"Why is any of this happening?" Uncle Morty asked. "I always saw Virtual Reality as a way to teach surgeons better methods to do delicate operations or bomb squads how to disarm delicate bombs. You guys have turned it into an Indiana Jones adventure."

"Fun, huh?" Kelly said, with just a hint of sarcasm. "But this time it's not our fault. Matthew Helbert's hidden one of his discoveries, and Tim's after it," she told him again. "We find it, and we're rich and famous; we don't, and we're milking cows for the rest of our lives. Plus, if we do find it we might even help a few people."

"I'm glad I'm here then," Uncle Morty said. "If Matthew developed it, you'll probably need me to figure out what it is and how to use it."

"But how are we going to get the crown?"

"You're not," the guy Tim had called Graham said, walking up to them. "That crown hangs there until we all drown in chocolate." Then he turned to the guards. "No one touches that crown. I'm going to take a detachment and go get that Tim-guy. He might just decide to blow up the dam anyway."

Uncle Morty studied the dam for a moment, "It's made out of something weird. Like fruitcake. What's behind the dam?" he asked.

"Chocolate—a sea of it. Hard to breathe under chocolate," Graham explained.

"Is the dam weak?"

"Not now. Fruitcake's the strongest building material we've got here. But it can be blown up."

"Well," said Uncle Morty, "we wouldn't want that now, would we."

Graham laughed softly. "While you stew here, we'll go make sure your friend there doesn't bother it."

A few minutes later Kelly, Gar, and Uncle Morty watched as about thirty Valley People headed off toward the dam and the trail that led to Tim.

"They look like they mean business," Gar said softly.

A moment later the three of them were alone with their five guards.

Sonya watched Tim from where she rested on the rise and longed to help him. That was what she'd been programmed to do, and now she couldn't do it. She'd also been programmed to do what was necessary to get her up and around the fastest. Her programming said a severe sprain required a certain amount of rest and cool, swirling water.

It was time to go to her favorite place and rest for a while.

In a place in the computer known only to computer characters, she found the computer address of her beloved water cavern. After softly repeating the address, she transported there. A moment later she sat in a secluded little alcove, dangling her injured leg in the cool, swirling water.

Back at Goody Land, Hammond Helbert watched Tim and the others from behind a chocolate boulder. His plan was unfolding nicely. He'd hurt that Tim-kid, scared that Kelly-girl to death, and beat her up a little. He had battered their uncle pretty well too. It wouldn't be long now until the final beating—the very final beating.

But Hammond did have a concern.

There was only about fifteen minutes until sunset. They would get suspicious if Tim didn't make it but was allowed to go forward anyway. Hammond took out his small terminal and punched in a couple of numbers. When the right display came up, he entered a couple more. He had slowed down the sun. Now the kid had twenty minutes. And if that wasn't enough, Hammond Helbert would slow the sun down again, maybe even wind it backward for a while.

Uncle Morty glanced around him. He, Kelly, and Gar were surrounded by five soldiers. Each was armed with a pretty sharp-looking spear and a grim, though bored, expression. The thirty soldiers who had gone after Tim were still visible in the distance. They'd just about reached the dam.

Uncle Morty eyed the crown. It still rested on the crudely carved moose head. For whatever reason, Tim needed that crown. And he, Kelly, and Gar needed to get away from these guys. There had to be a way to accomplish both. *You're a genius, stupid. Think of something!* Tim needed him—needed his help finding, deciphering, and using Matthew's discovery. *Okay,* Uncle Morty thought, *if you are the genius the treasure needs, figure out a way to escape with the crown! Lord, you're the real genius around here. What do you think?*

"You know, when I come back . . ." Gar began after studying the totem pole for a while.

"When?" Kelly said, her voice betraying some excitement. "You're coming back? Even after this?"

"Sure. And I was thinking. We could program those heads on the totem to entertain us. Sing songs, tell jokes—a balancing and tumbling act."

"We could make the moose a soprano."

A thought came to Uncle Morty.

He turned toward the moose, cocked his head as if he'd heard something, then took a step closer to it. A soldier in front of him, one with an exceptionally large nose, popped a spear up to block his path, but Uncle Morty brushed it aside, his eyes fixed on the moose head. "What?" Uncle Morty replied to the moose. He listened intently, then laughed. "They seem pretty clean to me."

"What? He said something?" Big Nose asked Uncle Morty, his eyes wide.

"He called you dirty fatheads," Uncle Morty explained, moving even closer to the moose. Turning back to the moose, he waited a moment, then replied, "No, I don't."

"Fatheads? Uh, don't what?" another soldier, this one with monster ears, asked.

A buzz erupted from the others. "What's going on?"

"He's talkin' to the moose."

"Moose don't talk. 'Specially that one."

"Did you hear anythin'?"

"No."

Confused, they all took a step toward Uncle Morty and the moose.

Uncle Morty told Big Nose, "He wonders if I hunt."

"I'd think he'd care more if you owned a chain saw," a bald guard pointed out.

"Maybe he don't know he's wood," one with saggy eyes said.

"What?"

"Moose asked if he hunts," Saggy Eyes related.

"The moose asked? I've cleaned that moose off every week for four years, and it never once asked me if I hunt—never asked me nothin'."

"Fatheads?" Monster Ears asked again. "Why would he call us fatheads?"

"I think we ought to get this guy back where he was," one with bushy brows suggested. He'd stayed a little back from everything.

Uncle Morty remained, his ear cocked toward the moose again. "I'm sure they would," he replied.

"Would what?" Big Nose asked, cocking his ear toward the moose as well.

"Greg, here, wants you guys to carry the totem out of the valley when the chocolate comes."

"Greg?" Saggy Eyes asked, confused. "Who's Greg?"

"The moose is Greg," Baldy said, setting him straight.

"But guys, he called us fatheads," Monster Ears pointed out, fingering his spear as if deciding whether to plant the point right at the end of the moose's nose.

"Greg?" Big Nose questioned. "What kind of name is that for a moose?"

"I had an Uncle Greg."

"Greg seems like an okay name."

"For a moose?"

"I haven't seen him talk and already he's got a name?"

"Maybe he talks in high-pitched sounds."

"Without moving his lips?"

"Maybe he's a ventriloquist."

"Right—and you're his dummy."

"But what's this about chocolate coming?" Bushy Brows asked, still hanging back in concern.

"I think I'm going to spear him," Monster Ears finally said, raising his spear as if to skewer the moose's considerable nose.

Uncle Morty calmly pulled the spear down. Stepping even closer to the moose, he appeared to listen intently. Then with an increasingly serious expression, he nodded. "Oh, yes, I'm sure they'd make that trade."

"What trade?" Big Nose asked, eyes narrow with the question.

"Simple really," Uncle Morty said. "You promise to carry

him and the totem out of the valley, and he'll tell you when the bomb is set to go off."

Their eyes popped and their jaws dropped. In near unison they gasped, "Bomb?" They were believers.

"Where?" Big Nose and Saggy Eyes asked together.

Slowly Uncle Morty turned toward the dam. As he turned, the guards did too.

"It's in the dam," Baldy gasped.

"How many cherries did they use?" Bushy Brows asked.

"Hundreds," Uncle Morty reported after listening for a moment to his friend Greg.

"Hundreds," they all gasped again.

"When will it explode?" Bushy Brows asked reverently, as if the question might hurry the explosion along.

"Well," Uncle Morty said, "in about ten minutes. Which doesn't give you much time to dig out the totem and carry it out of the valley."

"Come on," Monster Ears said. "This is a wooden moose—it's not even the head of a real moose. It can't talk. No way."

"What's up with her?" Bushy Brows asked, pointing at Kelly.

The others turned and were terrified by what they saw. Kelly's face was screwed up into a frightening mask. She shook. Her hands seemed to vibrate with a life of their own. "Please get us out of here," she said in a thin, vaporous voice. "I don't want to drown in chocolate. My uncle can talk to animal spirits. It's true. He has the gift. Please get us out of here." And then she screamed—it was a piercing, bloodcurdling scream.

That did it!

"I'm out o' here," Big Nose yelped.

"Me too."

"Where we going?" Bushy Brows asked, as confused as ever.

"The chocolate will eat away at the walls—we can't dig. We have to get to high ground."

"Come on. It's every man for himself."

And it was. All five took off in different directions, and within seconds Uncle Morty, Kelly, and Gar were left alone.

"Come on," Uncle Morty said. "Let's get that crown and find Tim."

"You were great," Gar said to Kelly.

Kelly smiled. "Maybe I shouldn't show you all of my secrets."

"Kelly," Uncle Morty interrupted, "I'll hoist you up, and you get it." Uncle Morty made a stirrup of his hand, and she stepped on it. She grabbed the chocolate crown and brought it down. The moment her foot touched the floor, another voice shouted from the cliffs. "How dare you try to invade the mountain country with that band of criminals?"

"He must be talking about Graham's troop going after Tim," Gar said.

"All agreements are off, Graham," the voice cried. "The dam comes down now."

At that instant an arc of huge, red cherries flew toward the crest of the dam, one after another as if fired from several catapults. As each struck, the fizzy-water within them caused a deafening pop and a portion of the fruitcake was ripped away.

"Oh my," Kelly gasped. "We need to do something—fast."

That's when they heard Tim's voice. They turned to find him standing on the top of the ice cream cliff maybe thirty feet above them. "I need the crown. The sun's about to go down."

"But we need to get out of here," Uncle Morty called back.

"If I don't get the crown we'll lose it all."

Kelly remembered something and began patting her pockets to find it. She pulled out her invention.

"Stand back," she said.

All but ignoring her, Gar exclaimed, "Look!" He pointed toward the dam. A section of it had given way, and a river of chocolate spilled over it. It splashed into the valley. It dug a deep hole in the valley but then broke over the edges in massive waves. It was heading right for them.

Kelly pointed her invention at the totem pole and cried, "Ferris wheel—a big Ferris wheel."

Surprised by her success, she watched as the totem instantly shot up a hundred feet. Two huge fans spun out and converged into the two wheels on either side. Seats appeared and connected the wheels.

"It'd better hurry," Uncle Morty said anxiously. "More of the dam's breaking off."

A sea of chocolate crashed over the weakened structure. In a high wave, the chocolate slammed into the village structures, flattening some, pushing others before it, inundating others. When the village was only a memory, the massive wall of frothy brown continued on relentlessly.

But the Ferris wheel was complete, and Kelly, Gar, and Uncle

Morty were aboard. The instant the safety bar was clamped into place the wheel began to turn.

"Faster, faster," whispered Gar.

"Please, God," muttered Kelly.

"We made it," cried Uncle Morty as the chair rose above the tidal wave of brown that washed below them.

But the sea of chocolate grabbed the wheel and ground it to a halt.

"Guys, I need that crown," Tim cried. "The sun." He pointed off toward the horizon and saw the sun only inches from touching it.

"Calm down, Tim," Uncle Morty fired back. "We've got an emergency here."

"We need to climb over to Tim," Kelly said. The Ferris wheel touched the edge of the cliff on which Tim stood, but their seat was on the opposite side of the wheel.

"We don't have time," Uncle Morty said, eying the long, narrow beam they would have to walk across.

"We might," Kelly said, pointing at the sun again. It looked higher than a minute ago, almost as if it had gone backward for a moment.

"Okay, let's go," Uncle Morty said reluctantly.

With the chocolate surging below them and with the dam threatening to unleash even more chocolate, enough perhaps to cause the Ferris wheel to crumble, Uncle Morty, Kelly, and Gar stood in the seat and took their first steps onto the cross beam.

Tim stationed himself at the opposite end of the beam waiting—impatiently. "Come on, guys—hurry."

"You're kidding, right?" Kelly fired back.

Grabbing whatever was near, they steadied themselves as they worked their way across the beam. It was Kelly first, Gar next, with Uncle Morty following. Gar and Uncle Morty seemed pretty steady, but Kelly moved slowly and deliberately as if each step might be her last—which she firmly believed.

Below the chocolate churned, battling the edges of the valley.

"Oh, no," Kelly gasped. "The dam!"

They all turned to see the remainder of the fruitcake crumble. A wall of chocolate advanced, rolling over the remainder of the dam and charging toward them.

"Let's go, Kelly," Gar said.

Kelly swallowed hard, said a quick prayer, and ran along the beam, her hands grabbing guide wires and beams rapidly—as fast as her feet.

The wall of chocolate struck the Ferris wheel. The base groaned and twisted upon impact, then the wheels tore apart, and the steel fell beneath the mighty waves.

Kelly, Gar, and Uncle Morty watched in amazement from the cliff. Uncle Morty, the last to reach the cliff, stepped off the Ferris wheel just as the steel girder buckled beneath his feet.

"You did really well, Kelly," Gar said.

"I was scared to death."

"You wouldn't know it."

"My crown. Give me the crown," Tim demanded.

Kelly took it from her head and handed it to him. In the excitement a couple of the crown's points had broken off. But that didn't matter.

Just as the sun dipped behind the mountains beyond the dam, Tim placed the crown on his head. "See, God wants me to succeed."

"Now what?" Uncle Morty asked.

"I don't know," Tim said. "Is there a note around someplace—anything that might tell us?"

"Not that I see," Kelly said after looking around.

Uncle Morty saw it this time. Not far from where they stood was the dark opening to a cave. Maybe six feet high, the opening was strikingly black against the white—unfathomable. "I don't recall seeing that before."

Tim didn't reply but walked toward the cave entrance. The others followed. Upon reaching the entrance, they peeked cautiously inside.

The walls glowed an eerie blue. They encased the delicate sound of water—dripping, some lapping at the cave walls. "There's a rowboat," Tim said, pointing.

Remaining cautious, they walked to it.

"A note," Gar pointed to the front of two seats.

Tim grabbed it and read it without allowing the others to see it. "Okay," he said. "I get half. You guys share the rest."

Uncle Morty didn't reply. He snatched the paper from Tim and read it himself. "This is it," he told Kelly and Gar. "It's at the end of this little stream here—we'll find a pool, and everyone in the boat—I guess that means all of us, Tim—"

Tim cringed. They were going to take what was his. He was

the one who spent the most time in VR. He was the one who did whatever it was that opened the doors to the treasure. He was the one who'd been shot, whipped, plastered with exploding cherries. He was the one who made everything work. Whatever lay at the end of this stream was *his*.

Morty went on. "We're all supposed to dive to the bottom of the pool and each bring up a portion of whatever it is. There will be red lights to indicate where the various pieces lie."

Tim said nothing. He took a seat at the midsection of the boat. Uncle Morty sat next to him while Gar and Kelly took the seat in the stern. Grabbing oars, Tim and Uncle Morty began to row.

CHAPTER 15

Sonya sensed the seconds and minutes ticking away as she sat soaking her leg in a secluded corner of her and Tim's water park. Each second that ticked away meant she was a second closer to being with Tim again. Maybe they'd be sitting here together again soon—in the cool cavern amid the constant rush and splash of the falls, enjoying the seclusion. After all, she and Tim were the only ones who knew about this place.

That's why she was shocked to hear a man laughing.

Although her ankle still registered pain, she yanked it from the water and rolled to a hiding place behind a nearby boulder.

The laughter continued, and a moment later its source came into view. Hammond Helbert. She had been programmed to recognize him long ago—all the computer characters had. Matthew, their beloved Matthew, wanted to know if his brother, Hammond, ever came into VR.

And there he was.

He stood by the edge of the pool, a small device in his hand. He was looking into the device's little screen and laughing. "Maybe I won't have to do anything to them," he finally said. "They're about to kill each other without my help. Christians. They're all alike."

What was she to do? Matthew wasn't in VR. She couldn't contact him. Then, as if struck by the lightning of decision, she knew precisely what she was supposed to do. Overcoming the pain in her ankle by sheer will, she pulled herself into an even tighter ball behind the rocks and watched—and waited.

Hammond now lay on a flat rock, stomach down, his chin inches from the water, staring into its depths. He'd taken a small fishbowl from the VR tool crib. Holding it just above the water's surface, he waited—patiently at first, but impatiently now. Whatever humor he'd seen in the argument between the Morty-guy, the Kelly-girl, and the Tim-boy was gone. He now had to catch some fish, and he had to do it quickly—his plan depended on it.

At just the right moment, he dipped the bowl into the water and came up with three goldfish. They wouldn't be goldfish for long! Setting the bowl on the rock beside him, he pulled out his little terminal. Entering a couple of quick commands, he found the fishes characteristics. VR had preprogrammed a number of different kinds of fish, but they were not the kind Hammond wanted. Taking care to make no errors, he entered new characteristics for the goldfish.

"Teeth: sharp, jagged; jaw: jutting."

The fish in the bowl suddenly had menacing teeth protruding from ugly, jutting jaws.

He changed their diet from small plants and algae to meat.

The fish in the bowl began swimming about frantically as if searching for prey.

He gave them the ability to sense their prey from a long way off.

The fish in the bowl pointed their menacing teeth and jutting jaw at him and pushed their jaws against the bowl as if trying to swim through the glass to attack him.

He had created his piranha.

Then he entered the "duplicate" command followed by the number: ten thousand.

The three piranha in the bowl became six, then twelve, then twenty-four, forty-eight, then they doubled again and again. They filled the bowl, then flopped out of the bowl and slapped about on the rock. Terror-stricken, Hammond kicked the bowl, and it sailed several feet out into the water, then he kicked the few fish on the rock into the water. But one of them was waiting for him. It latched onto his foot and bit. A pain like he'd never known shot up his leg. VR was simulating the bite of a piranha in the only way it knew how, by turning on all the juice. Hammond wondered what it would be like to have a thousand of those jaws gnawing on him—or rather, gnawing on the uncle and the three kids. Reacting instinctively, Hammond brought his other shoe down hard upon the fish and smashed it on the rock. The pain ceased. He kicked the dead fish into the water.

The instant it hit water the surface boiled as the other piranha attacked the carcass. Seconds later the surface was calm again, the fish bones sinking to the bottom of the pool.

"Wonderful," Hammond whispered. "Absolutely wonderful. If one could produce such pain in me, what will ten thousand produce in them? The president will certainly be upset with me this time." His laughter echoed off the stone walls. But, not wanting to be heard, he stopped. Then, after preparing a couple more things, he climbed to a tall ledge, one that would have made a good diving platform, and waited secretively. It was a great place from which to watch—just enough cover from surrounding rocks and just far enough out over the water to see all four of the glowing red lights—he'd be able to see everything below the water's surface.

Oh, what a show this was going to be. What a show! Almost as good as a televised execution.

回

Tim and Uncle Morty paddled silently. The argument was over—or at least the loud words were, but Tim's hard feelings would never be appeased. At least that's what he decided. Uncle Morty had made it very clear that without him, no matter what the discovery was, Tim would probably not be able to understand it. Then Kelly had chimed in about how they had been beaten up trying to get to him and how she and Gar should share. Tim felt a twinge of guilt, but only a twinge, and countered that it was because he'd been so faithful programming VR that he was the one chosen. Gar shouldn't share because he was only here by chance and, being the president's son, he had enough anyway. After all, it was he, Tim, who tripped whatever switch Matthew had put in VR to reveal the path to the treasure.

Finally Tim decided that he'd just have to wait and take charge when they found Matthew's secret.

"I like boating," Gar said. "You guys live near a lake, don't you? I remember seeing it when we were landing."

"Hundred and forty miles of shore line," Kelly said with a note of pride. "We have a little cove we swim in."

"Maybe when we get out of this we can take a walk down there?"

Kelly smiled. "Sure. But there's another place down there I'd like you to see—a better place to walk through."

"Pay attention now," Uncle Morty said. "We're coming to a cavern. I think I hear waterfalls."

Tim nodded. "That's it."

As the rush of water grew to a roar, they emerged from the small cave and glided gently into the deep, sky blue pool. Cascading from the walls and rocks all around them were the waterfalls. They struck the water tumultuously, but for some reason known only to the computer, the surface of the pool was calm only a short distance from the water's impact.

"Wow!" Kelly gasped. "This is awesome."

"It's like a water park," Gar said, his eyes wide with awe.

Even Uncle Morty was impressed. His mouth dropped as he looked all about him. The glow of the walls sent a magical assortment of colors shimmering through the falling water and resulting mist—a rainbow. "The thunder of the falls brings excitement," he said. "I never thought VR could produce something like this—even if told to."

"It did it on its own," Tim said. But not to be sidetracked, he began to scan the water's depths. "The note said we're to look for red lights."

"In a minute," Kelly said. "I want to check this place out."

"I want to see what's down there," Tim insisted.

"It's not good to be so anxious," Uncle Morty injected.

"This isn't about good or bad," Tim protested, his physical and emotional wounds still festering. "This is about being rich and famous and taking what Matthew gives us and making the most of it. That's what this is all about."

"You're going off the deep end about this thing, Tim," Uncle Morty said.

"Deep end? I'm the one who owns whatever is down there. I can go off the deep end if I want."

Before Tim finished his sentence they all heard Kelly say, "Red lights."

Hammond Helbert nearly cheered. Soon the water would boil, and those four twits would fry inside their black suits.

Sonya was no longer hiding behind the boulder. She inched her way from rock to rock. She knew she could simply warn Tim and the others, but that wouldn't accomplish Matthew's purpose, and right now, Matthew's purpose was her top priority. Long ago Matthew had programmed her that way.

Kelly, Tim, Gar, and Uncle Morty leaned over the side of the boat. "I see it too," Gar said, pointing.

"Where?" Uncle Morty asked, his voice tight.

"Under that ledge over there."

"Look, another one," Kelly said. "That's two. Are there more?"

"There's another—that's three."

Gar saw the fourth. "Four lights. Four of us. How would it know there are four of us?"

"It's a computer," Tim said sarcastically. "Computers know everything. I still think I should go down. I don't need you people."

"Then why did you leave us that note on the screen at Uncle Morty's and that other note at the parachute?" Kelly asked.

Hammond Helbert cringed. All Tim had to say was "I didn't leave any notes," and his whole plan would fall apart. They would realize that something was wrong. They might even realize it was he, Hammond Helbert, at work to destroy them.

"This is mine," Tim said as if he'd not even heard Kelly's question. "Nothing matters but that." He positioned himself to dive into the pool. He would have, too, had not Uncle Morty grabbed him by the shirt.

"Without us you wouldn't have even gotten here. We're all going in."

Hammond couldn't believe his ears. They hadn't discovered his part in tricking them, and they were going to leap in—to their dooms. He loved it. He wanted to cheer again.

Suddenly the world turned on him.

"Hammond Helbert!"

The sharp female voice caught him completely off guard. Surprised, he stood and turned. "I've got a message for you from Matthew," Sonya said, and before he could mutter a word of protest she tossed the message at him—a thirty-pound rock.

Hammond instinctively caught it.

The next instant, Sonya threw herself at him and pushed. Hammond Helbert, his face stamped with shock, toppled over the edge. Halfway to the water, he started screaming. Boulder in hand, he couldn't press his palm button to escape before he hit the water.

Having heard the voice above them, Uncle Morty, Tim, Kelly, and Gar saw Hammond plunge beneath the surface. The splash was tremendous—but more tremendous was the sudden tumult in the water; it boiled frantically.

Sonya peered over the ledge. "Matthew's programming," she said simply.

"Look! He had the pool stocked with piranha," Uncle Morty said, his voice a mix of fear, awe, and relief.

Tim's eyes widened. As suddenly as any realization had ever struck him before, several things collided and fused in his mind. "I know where he is," he cried. "Where he really is."

Without another word Tim pushed his palm button.

The water world faded and his visor rose.

Unzipping his black suit as quickly as he could, he was taken aback when he saw everyone in the computer room—his father, his mother, the Secret Service agents.

"What's this all about, Tim? You have responsibilities on the farm—"

"Dad, believe me, I agree with you, but there's no time." He turned to the Secret Service agents and said, "I know where he is. I know where Hammond Helbert is. Come on."

Tim ran from the computer room, and two Secret Service agents followed. As they disappeared off the front porch, Kelly and Gar emerged from VR, and a moment later Uncle Morty did as well.

"What's going on?" John Craft asked.

"Hammond Helbert's being eaten by virtual piranha—something he had planned for us. Tim says he knows where he is."

Tim and the agents ran across the fields toward the deserted Higgins farmhouse. This is where Hammond Helbert had to be. That strange reflector on the windmill—the one that had blinded Tim the morning before when he was rounding up the cows—it was a microwave dish! It had to be. Helbert needed a high place to put it, and only he had a reason to put anything upon the Higgins' roof. None of the local farmers would have done that. Even if they had a reason, they never would have trespassed on the old farm. It was thrilling for Tim to know something so clearly. And it was even more thrilling to see that he was right as he and the Secret Service agents approached. Tim only pointed up at the dish as they ran toward the dilapidated, time-ravaged old house.

Mounting the old porch, they took no time to catch their breath, and the agents burst through the rotting front door. Finding nothing but cobwebs, they waited for Tim, who ran past them to the cellar door. He threw it open and ran down the stairs, the agents right behind him.

As much as Tim wanted Hammond Helbert to feel the excruciating sting of justice, he found it hard to want anyone, even Hammond, to go through what he was going through now. Still in the black suit, unable to escape because of the fierce attack, Hammond stood writhing in anguish.

As the agents pulled their guns, Tim rushed over to him and pressed his palm. The instant the visor rose, the suit went limp and Hammond collapsed. He'd fallen into his own trap, and he had paid dearly.

CHAPTER 16

Y ou got him," Gar praised Tim as the ambulance with Hammond Helbert in it drove off.

"He nearly got us," Tim said. "And it's my fault he came so close."

Uncle Morty wrapped an arm around Tim's shoulder. "I didn't help matters much. I have to admit, I could see those millions and all that recognition too."

John Craft gave his son a gentle pat on his back. There would be time to talk later.

Actually there wasn't much time at all. The word got out somehow that something major was up, and before long four news vans were parked in front of the barn, and the national news people were on the phone telling anyone who would listen that their vans were on the way.

After a quick discussion between the Secret Service and the president, Bill Harkin, Gar was given his orders. "Get out of there, son. Now!"

Kelly's heart sank. They were supposed to have that walk by the lake, and she had planned to steer him over to those abandoned fruit trees—her secret place. He might have even stayed for dinner before heading off to resume his anti-gang tour.

Now all that dissolved, and she was reduced to saying a quick, unfulfilled good-bye and waving at him as the parade of three limousines pulled out.

She did get a call a moment later from his car phone, though. "You really are an exciting date," he said.

"I'm too young to date."

"Me too," and they laughed. "Oh, I almost forgot. When I saw that you'd made me the White Knight—I kind of liked that."

"He was my Prince Charming," she confided.

"I probably won't see you for a while."

"I know. But I'll see you on TV sometimes."

"It's hard to play Jenga over the phone."

"Take care, Gar. Call me if you get the chance. I'd like that."

"If I'm on TV or something and you see me scratch my nose, I'm saying hi. Okay?"

"Okay," said Kelly. "Have a good flight, and I'll see you later."

"'Bye, Kelly."

She hung up and instantly ran upstairs. Finding her pressed white rose, she held it for a while until the ache in her heart dulled.

"Kelly," her dad called up to her. "The reporters are finished with Tim and your uncle. They want to talk to you."

Knowing that she would have to mention Gar and also knowing that neither Gar nor his father would like that, she called back to her father, "Not interested."

Not long after Kelly and Tim finished the afternoon milking, Uncle Morty joined them for dinner. When apple pie and coffee were brought out, Uncle Morty leaned back in his chair, sipped June Craft's coffee appreciatively, and said, "I've decided to go back to work."

Everyone's ears perked up.

"You have?" John Craft asked disbelievingly. "With the lawn mower race over I'm sure there's a frog jumping contest somewhere to capture your attention."

"Maybe," Uncle Morty began, "but I've decided my retirement's over. The Lord has given me a brain and imagination. Nothing like Tim's here," he laughed—they all laughed, "but some. I don't want to go back to work for the government, but I've met this lady—the one who beat me in the lawn mower race—who owns a computer software company. I thought I could help her put together Christian stories for kids using the latest technology—CD ROM, for example. I've got some money to help kick things off. Maybe someday I'll catch up to you,

John—someday I'll be the Christian man you are. And maybe I'll end up with some of those responsibilities you speak so fondly of."

Still a little shocked by his brother's announcement, John Craft said nothing for a while. Tim thought he detected a tear in the corner of his father's eye, but it never broke loose. "You'll do well at that," John finally said. "I'm still thinking about putting a fax in my tractor—start taking advantage of technology. Every tractor needs a fax." Then his expression became serious. The kids knew that expression. It meant he had something important to say. He didn't disappoint them. "I know you kids can hardly wait to get off the farm," he started, the words difficult for him. They started to protest, but he waved their protests away. "Let's talk about hopes and dreams—fantasies and careers."

"If it's about all that programming . . ." Tim said.

"It is," John Craft said. "Dreams are good, you guys. God gives us dreams—sometimes. The other guy can, too, but when our dreams and fantasies are legal and God honoring, they're from the Lord. They become our goals and objectives—things to work toward. But most of our lives are 'here and now.' The Christian life is a balancing act."

"Can I say something, Dad?" Tim asked respectfully.

His father nodded.

"Those dreams I programmed were things I thought I wanted—maybe still want—recognition, being in charge, winning. But it's no good when they take over, when they interfere with what we should be doing today. Plus, I found out I liked the struggle sometimes more than the winning. It was fun when the computer gave me things I didn't know about—I guess like God does in real life. It made success that much better."

"Sometimes our 'wants' are given to us just so we experience the struggle to achieve them—when we struggle we grow. Building this farm, raising you kids, serving my Lord is a struggle—and I grow every day because of it. Sometimes the struggle becomes the goal—living our lives with integrity, with honesty."

"We all got pretty greedy there," Kelly said, pushing her pie away half eaten.

"Dreams mean nothing without Jesus," Tim said, as if he'd hit a bedrock notion.

"Our dreams are his gifts. This farm, you, your mom, being a farmer, father, husband—those are all gifts, and if I treat them well, maybe he'll give me more to do—more dreams. Keep in mind that there's nothing more rewarding than to accomplish the tasks the Lord has given us. You two seem to have great imaginations and an ability to program. Maybe you ought to talk to Uncle Morty; sounds like he could use you in that new venture of his. In your *spare* time—that is."

Uncle Morty laughed. "I guess I'm the money man—I can do whatever I like. And I'd like to talk to my new boss and see if she approves."

John Craft eyed his daughter for a moment. "What did *you* learn?" he asked.

She shrugged. "I guess what you said," she offered, but she seemed preoccupied.

"Is there something else?" her mother asked.

"It's nothing," Kelly said insincerely.

回

Tim was up in his room alone, and the house was quiet. Dad, Mom, and Uncle Morty were on the porch having their last cups of coffee. The sky was dark, the stars a wash of sparkles—so much out there and God was bigger than all of it. *Yet he loves me*, Tim said to himself. *He's given me so much—and most of all himself—to help me grow as I work and struggle through life.*

回

While Tim lay thinking, Kelly climbed out of her bedroom window, grabbed the limb of a conveniently overhanging tree, and climbed down. Several minutes later she was climbing into the VR suit. After the visor came down and the virtual world came alive, she ran to her Harley and climbed aboard. Firing it up, she rode as fast as she could. She didn't like trying to jump the Grand Canyon, and she liked it less when the jets ran out of fuel and she ended up plunging a million feet. The ledge she landed on seemed endless. When she found Tim's cave, the caverns seemed endless too. But all that didn't matter much. She was on a personal mission.

"Sonya," she called to the walls. She hiked further. "Sonya!"

"Up here," finally came Sonya's voice from high on a cavern wall.

Kelly looked up and saw her standing there.

"What do you want?" Sonya said, her voice just a bit harsh.

"I'll be right up." Actually it took Kelly a while, but finally she stood next to Sonya, and a few minutes later they both sat on the edge of the crystal blue pool, the waterfalls rushing all around them.

"Okay—why are you here?" Sonya asked her.

"I was saved by a cartoon," Kelly told her. "I'm having trouble dealing with that."

"Why?"

"I don't know. But I wanted to talk to you about it."

"Would you like it better if I hadn't saved you?"

"No. Saving me was a good thing. But I don't like that you did it somehow."

"Why?"

"Saving me makes you real. I mean, I couldn't be saved by something not real. That just feels funny somehow."

"What's funny?"

"If you're real I have to like you—love you. God says I have to love you. But you're only a cartoon."

"I was created by Matthew. If I was created, how can I not exist?"

"But why did you save us?" Kelly asked, as if the answer was important.

"I had to. Actually, I wasn't so much saving you as dealing with Hammond Helbert. But with you guys, particularly Tim, in trouble, I had to deal with Hammond without harming you. I was just doing what Matthew, my creator, wanted me to. As my creator, he sort of owns me."

"I guess we're all supposed to do that—what our creator tells us to."

"You don't like me, do you?" Sonya said.

"I just think it's stupid that Tim likes you so much."

"Tim likes me?"

"But then you saved my life."

"He likes me?"

"Yeah, he likes you." Kelly peered into the blue pool. "Are there still piranha in there?"

"Sure. Hey, what's it like out there?" Sonya asked.

"Okay—reality's okay."

"Are there other boys like Tim out there?"

"Tim's one of a kind. But there's a lot of others. Maybe too many."

"Really? What are they like?"

"Like—guys—you know. There's really only one good one. And he's two thousand miles away right now."

"Lots of guys? Wow. How could I get out there?"

"I think I want you safely in here."

"Why?"

"I've got all the competition I need out there."

"But maybe you could think of something."

Kelly smiled at her. "Fat chance."

ABOUT THE AUTHOR

Bill Kritlow was born in Gary, Indiana, and moved to northern California when he was nine. He now resides in southern California with his wife, Patricia. They have three daughters and five grandchildren. Bill is also a deacon at his church.

After spending twenty years in large-scale computing, Bill recently changed occupations so that he could spend most of the day writing—his first love. His hobbies include writing, golf, writing, traveling, and taking long walks to think about writing. *Backfire* follows Bill's first two books in the Virtual Reality Series, *A Race Against Time* and *The Deadly Maze*. He has also written *Driving Lessons* and *Crimson Snow*.

Read other Virtual Reality adventures
with Kelly and Tim Craft in

A Race Against Time

and

The Deadly Maze